An Elemental Wind

Carol R. Ward

An Elemental Wind
ISBN 978-1937477950
An Elemental Wind Copyright © 2011 Carol R. Ward
Published by Brazen Snake Books

Cover art by Heidi Sutherlin

Dedication

To Jamie, Heidi, and Karin — the best friends I never met.
You guys rock!

Acknowledgments

A special acknowledgment to Jamie DeBree for her
continued support and encouragement. This book
wouldn't have been possible without her.

Chapter One

There were no moons orbiting Temus, but the native predators didn't need light to hunt, which made it dangerous to be anywhere but the T'tenet cities at night. The landing field and loading docks were dangerous for a different reason and this danger was in no way mitigated by the light streaming from the window of the meeting house located just at the edge of the field. In fact, the predators of Temus gave the swath of light a wide birth.

Chaney fidgeted in the poorly ventilated interior. Not only were the T'tenet hideous to look at, they smelled repulsive too. He needed air, badly. How could anyone trust these creatures – muddy green warty skin, bulging eyes, bulbous lips – they looked like giant amphibians. Already one crew member from the Burning Comet had vanished; they needed to find out what happened to him. He wished his skills extended to linguistics, he'd love to know what the T'tenet crowded in the back were muttering about.

"Chaney," Cap's voice was barely a whisper, but it was enough to draw the young navigator to one side.

"It's a set up. Use the E.T.T. to warn Vida to get the ship fired up. We need to get out of here. I'll try to warn Tavis."

A barely discernible nod, then Chaney bit down with his molars.

"I read you, Chaney," Vida's disembodied voice whispered in his mind. "Hook-up complete. Ready for thought transference."

He relayed the captain's message, eyes flickering over the restless T'tenet. Tavis, their interpreter, and the T'tenet leader were in a heated argument. Vida signaled the message received and understood.

A sudden explosion rocked the meeting house. For a moment, everyone froze, then bedlam ensued.

"Run for it!" Cap shouted.

The meeting house was on fire. T'tenet and human alike sought the safety of the darkness only to be caught in a backwash of laser fire. Chaney dove behind a stack of barrels on the loading dock; Cap skidded to a stop behind a storage shed. The shots from the laser continued as more T'tenet appeared out of the night.

"Tavis, Chaney, where are you?" The captain spoke as loud as he dared into his communicator.

"I'm over by the loading dock, Cap," Chaney answered.

"Where's Tavis?"

"The T'tenet got him right before the building exploded."

Cap swore softly. The meeting house was blazing. Hideous screams came from the T'tenet still trapped inside. The stench was nearly overwhelming. Those lucky enough to escape, T'tenet and human alike, were being picked off by laser fire from the unknown assailant.

"We have to get to the ship before they light the beacons," Cap whispered urgently into his communicator.

"Between the sniper and the T'tenet that's not going to be easy." Chaney squinted into the darkness, trying to pinpoint where the shots were coming from.

Several of the ugly, toad-like creatures were firing indiscriminately into the darkness. They didn't seem to care who they hit as long as they hit something. The green of their weapons fire was met with blue from the sniper's laser.

"Listen," Chaney suggested. "You're on the right side of the field. You should be able to make it back to the ship. If I'm not right behind you, lift off without me."

"We need to get that sniper. I need to know if our mission's been compromised."

"What if he's T'tenet? This could all be nothing more than a power struggle between factions."

"He's not. Trust me, I have a hunch."

"I'll get him," Chaney promised grimly.

"Don't kill him, try and take him prisoner."

Chaney eased himself down off the dock and was lost in the darkness. He kept low, circling around to a point behind where he believed the shots to be coming from. He could see only vague shapes - barrels and dead T'tenet - until Cap made a break for the Burning Comet.

A blue flare, from a laser on low charge, missed the captain by a breath. Chaney made out a figure crouched behind a barrel, almost right under him.

With a soft rasp that couldn't be heard over the other sounds of the night, he pulled out his blaster and placed it in the center of the sniper's back. The figure started, then slowly rose. With his free hand, Chaney disarmed him and, indicating he would do well to remain silent, pointed him in the general direction of the Burning Comet.

Twice they stumbled over dead T'tenet in an effort to avoid live ones. The landing field was strewn with them. The prisoner stopped dead when he caught sight of the cruiser.

Chaney prodded him and the man whirled and hissed something in an alien tongue. He was a good deal shorter and lighter than Chaney but his stance proved him ready for a fight.

"Don't be a fool," Chaney said. "By morning the T'tenet will have slaughtered every human left on Temus. I don't know how you got here, but the Comet's your only chance."

Without warning, the sniper swung out, catching Chaney on the side of the jaw with his fist. Chaney cursed as he felt the E.T.T. fracture. It was an expensive piece of equipment and the third time he'd lost one this way. He barely caught the other first with one hand before it could connect as well. Damn, this sniper was fast! A move intended to twist the sniper's arm behind his back gained him a painful kick in the shins.

The navigator lost both his patience and temper altogether. He put all his force behind his clenched fist. It met the man's jaw with an audible crack and he dropped like a stone. Chaney grimaced and shook his hand. He had to admit though, as he swung the sniper over his shoulder, the little guy had guts.

The ship was fired up and ready to go as he sprinted up the ramp, ducking through the air lock as it sealed itself.

"That was cutting it close, Chaney." Vida's voice came over the intercom. "Blake wants you to take the prisoner to Nigel."

Chaney tightened his grip on his mud-covered burden and continued on his way.

"Nigel," he called, laying his charge down on one of the examining tables of the med-lab, "could you take a look at my hand? I think it's broken. And the E.T.T. will need replacing."

"That was the last Esper Thought Transfer we had on board, and at the rate you've been going through them I doubt the captain will replace it this time." The medical officer appeared from another room and clucked over Chaney's hand. "What did you do this time?"

"He's got an unaccountably hard jaw."

Nigel peered over his shoulder in the direction his thumb indicated. "He?"

The light of the med-lab revealed what the Temus night had kept hidden. The slender, feisty sniper was a woman, not a man. She was thin to the point of extreme. Her hair was tucked under the collar of her ill-fitting clothes. Little else could be discerned under the heavy layer of wet, grey mud that covered her from head to toe, but it was definitely a woman's form lying on the table.

Chaney's astonishment was comical, but he recovered quickly. "I guess I'd better inform the captain of this, right away."

Nakeisha woke to the sound of muted voices but kept her eyes closed, assessing her situation. There was softness beneath her, a softness she had not felt in too long a time. The air filling her lungs was clean and fresh with the faint, antiseptic smell of a medical facility. She must be on the ship she'd been shown.

Running a mental inventory she decided she was uninjured, except for where she'd been struck on the jaw, and unrestrained. Her head was foggy but that was probably due more to the lack of food, and exhaustion, than anything that had been done to her. Though her resources were low she could still fight if she had to.

Human voices, drawing closer. How long had it been since she'd heard a human speak?

"I think she's coming 'round."

"I'll let the captain know."

There was a whisper of movement and she felt someone near her. A touch on her arm – the sting of an injection. In a panic her eyes shot open.

"Relax," a gentle voice soothed. "It was just a mild stimulant. It won't harm you."

Her eyes flicked from the man standing beside the bed, to the furnishings of the room, then back to the man. He was of medium height and build, dressed in medical green. Shaggy red hair touched the collar of his uniform. His eyes were brown with just the faintest hint of lines around them to suggest his good nature.

He smiled. "My name is Nigel. I'm the ship's doctor." Reaching for a control behind her he said, "Don't be alarmed, I'm just going to raise your back support so you won't feel at such a disadvantage when the captain gets here. He'll want to ask you a few questions."

There was a hum of hydraulics and with a smooth movement the surface she was laying on reshaped itself, raising her back so she was sitting more or less upright. Her eyes flicked back to her surroundings. Yes, she was definitely in a medical facility. Someone, presumably the doctor, had washed the worst of the mud off her and dressed her in a shapeless synthetic garment of a paler green than his uniform.

She looked at him questioningly.

"I'm afraid there was no saving the clothes you were wearing," he said ruefully.

Movement in the door to the facility pulled her attention away. The captain was a big man, tall and broad, with a hint of grey in his otherwise brown hair and beard. He had an air of command about him which was how she was able to pick him out from the four people who entered the medical facility.

"She's awake," Nigel informed them, "but I don't know for how long."

"Understood," the captain said.

He seated himself on a stool beside the examination bed which brought him down more or less to eye level. She understood that he was trying to put her at ease, but she wasn't fooled. The others ranged themselves behind him, far enough away to appear harmless but close enough to act should she prove to be dangerous.

"My name is Blake Alcott," the big man told her. "I'm the Captain of the Burning Comet. You've already met Nigel, our doctor, and behind me is Chaney, our navigator, Vida, my second in command; and Libby, the ship's communications officer."

Her eyes flicked to the others.

Chaney was tall and lean, with not an ounce of surplus fat. His face might have almost been handsome, but for the tribal scars he bore on his right cheek. The black eyes under the bushy eyebrows gave nothing of his thoughts away.

Vida was just as tall as Chaney, although whip cord slender. Her blue eyes showed curiosity, more than anything, and her blond hair was pulled back tightly from her face and confined in a bun.

Libby was of medium height and build. Though her brown eyes and hair might be called ordinary, there was nothing ordinary about her features. She was an incredibly beautiful woman.

"Let's start with something simple, shall we?" Blake asked after giving her a moment to look the others over. "What's your name?"

It would be so easy to pretend she couldn't understand Universal, but she sensed no evil from these people and chose to answer instead. "I am Nakeisha Windsinger."

"Windsinger? I've never heard of such a planet."

The ones called Chaney and Vida exchanged a glance behind the captain's back.

"It is not a planet, it is what I am."

"Where are you from?"

"It does not matter. You will not have heard of it." If he had, she was in serious trouble.

"Designation?"

"I do not have one." She genuinely regretted having to add to the frustration the captain was starting to feel.

"Everyone has to have a designation," Vida said gently, trying to put her at ease.

"I do not."

"We'll let that go for now," Blake said to her. "You're not on trial here. Why were you shooting at us down there?"

"I was not shooting at you," she said indignantly. She didn't even know these people, why would she attack them? "I was aiming for the Toadies."

"Toadies?"

She tensed up, unable to mask the bitterness in her voice. "The T'tenet. We had some unfinished business."

"I don't suppose you feel inclined to tell us what kind of business?"

Nakeisha let her silence speak for her.

"If you don't have a designation, then how did you get to Temus?" Libby asked suddenly.

"I stowed away on a T'tenet freighter." A wave of weakness swept through her. She drew on the last of her reserves, unwilling to show a disadvantage in front of these strangers.

"A scrounger," Chaney said in disgust.

Her eyes cut towards him. He was very judgmental, this one, but that might work in her favor. There were definite advantages to being thought of as nothing more than a space tramp.

"Not necessarily," Vida broke in. "No matter how high you're designated it's not easy to secure a passage to Temus, unless of course you have your own ship."

"When was the last time you had a decent meal, or a decent night's sleep?" Nigel asked.

She shrugged. Though she refused to appear weak, she was not above playing on their sympathy. She let her eyes drift close.

"Captain, I move that we delay further questioning until Nakeisha's had a chance to rest. We're not going to get coherent answers from her while she's on the verge of exhaustion."

Blake hesitated, torn between the sense of Nigel's suggestion and needing answers. Nakeisha didn't wait to hear his reply but let the darkness take her away.

Chapter Two

Chaney made his way quickly down the corridor and into his quarters, engaging the privacy lock behind him. It wasn't that he didn't trust his fellow crew members, it was just force of habit from his academy days. It was always the lessons learned the hard way that were the most difficult to forget.

The command crew quarters on the Burning Comet were generous, by any standards, but right now Chaney found them claustrophobic. He paced restlessly, from the sitting room to the bedroom and back again. What was wrong with him?

A thin, sharp-featured face filled his mind. That sniper, Nakeisha, she disturbed his hard won serenity. He snagged the bottle of Hyrodian brandy from its shelf on his way by and then slumped down in his favorite chair.

Seeing her in the med-lab had been disquieting. She was smaller than he remembered, much thinner. He felt a twinge of guilt that he had struck someone so small and helpless. The livid bruise on her jaw was the only color to her other than her dark hair. Even her eyes were a pale grey. He uncorked the bottle and raised it to his lips.

Chaney snorted at his own thoughts. Small she may be, but she'd proved she was far from helpless. There was something to be admired in the fighting skill she'd shown. That must be what this feeling was, admiration for the skill of a fellow warrior. Not unlike the women of his own tribe. He took another deep pull from the bottle.

There was a crackle of static, then: "Chaney, Libby, report to the lounge."

Chaney corked the bottle with a sigh. No rest for the wicked, he thought as he levered himself out of the chair. He'd heard that somewhere but damned if he could remember where.

Nigel and Vida were already waiting with the captain when Chaney reached the lounge, Libby close on his heels. They seated themselves at the table and waited.

"We've got some decisions to make people," the captain wasted no time in getting started. "It's down to just the five of us. Do we turn back or continue with our mission?"

They'd started with a crew of twelve, a small enough crew for a master-class cruiser, but given the nature of their mission for the Pan-Galactic Council, Blake had seen no reason for a larger crew.

Vida frowned. "I dislike leaving a task unfinished."

"As do I," Libby agreed.

"Chaney?"

Chaney drummed his fingers on the table. "Seven of us have died. We would dishonor their memory if we were to turn back now."

"I concur," Nigel said.

"All right, we're agreed then," the captain said with approval. "Any suggestions on our next move?"

"The documents that led us to Temus were Tersic in origin," Libby said. "Maybe we should try the Great Library on Tersic."

"It would be well if it gives us the break we're looking for," Chaney said.

"What about our guest?" Vida asked.

They looked at Nigel.

Nigel's normal cheerfulness vanished. "I did a full scan on her . . . I'm keeping her unconscious for the next twenty-four hours to ensure she gets proper rest."

They waited patiently.

He sighed and slid a medical pad towards the captain. "It's all here in my report."

The captain glanced down at the pad and then looked up sharply. "You're sure about this?"

"Not that I've had much experience in such things, but yes, I'm sure."

"What is it?" Chaney asked impatiently.

The medical pad was slid in his direction. He read it, blanched, and read it again.

"But – who did this? The T'tenet?"

"We have no way of knowing, unless she cares to talk about it," Nigel said grimly. "And I, for one, do not care to question her too closely. There's more," he continued. "When she was still semi-conscious she started speaking. I have no idea what she was saying but I made a recording of it."

He set the recorder on the table and pressed the play button.

"It's an Ilezie dialect," Libby said after a few moments. "Few humans attempt to learn it and even fewer are able to master it. She speaks it like an Ilezie."

"Can you translate?" the captain asked.

Libby's brow furrowed in concentration. She listened to the recording once through then played it back, translating as it played.

"They did not know. I was strong E.Z. With your training I kept silent. Pain . . . so much pain."

Nakeisha's voice on the recording died to a whisper.

"The secret is safe."

Libby strained to hear and shook her head. "Something about coming too far to go back and protection."

There was a pause in the recording, then Nakeisha continued in a stronger voice. "Don't leave me E.Z., I can't do this alone!"

After that was only silence.

"What kind of trouble is she mixed up in?" Chaney asked. She was so much more than she appeared.

"More importantly, what kind of impact is this going to have on our mission?" Vida asked.

Blake looked at Nigel. "You have your twenty-four hours, doctor. But we'll need to question her as soon as she's strong enough."

The doctor kept Nakeisha in the sickbay for another day. She accepted his orders with an outward show of docility, but inside she seethed. Every parsec this ship traveled took her further from her revenge. She couldn't believe she allowed herself to be taken so easily.

Nakeisha paced the confines of the room she'd been given after the doctor finally released her. She should be resting, gathering her strength, planning her next move. Instead, she paced.

She was safe for the moment but knew better than to count on her luck holding out. This had been an ill-fated trip from the beginning. She wished she'd never left the home world.

Is that any way for an Elemental to be thinking?

The disembodied voice stopped her in her tracks.

"What—who—" She could feel another presence in the room with her.

Be at peace, child.

Nakeisha sank down on the closest chair. "I must be ill, I could have sworn—"

You're neither ill nor mad, the voice said impatiently. *Now pay attention.*

"E.Z.?"

Yes, it's me, child. The ship you are on is going to Tersic. You need to go with them. Once you're there you must get to the Great Library.

"But—you're dead," Nakeisha said, bewildered. She glanced around the room as though expecting to see him standing beside her.

There's dead and then there's dead. You know only a fraction of my power, child.

"Why are you speaking in my head? Where are you?"

There was a slight pause before E.Z. answered. *I have been with you since your Tespiro when you became a woman. You are an Illarie.*

"An *Illarie?* Why was I never told?"

There was another hesitation before he answered. *It was decided it would be in your best interest if you did not know.*

Nakeisha got up and went over to the view port. She fought back the tears that threatened to spill over. "If I am your *Illarie*, then why haven't you spoken to me before?" she asked finally, staring out at the stars.

I tried, the voice said gently. *But you were too angry. You could not hear me over your rage.*

"Oh." Shame filled her. She had lashed out blindly, forgetting her training, forgetting her hard won serenity. So many T'tenet dead by her hand, she hadn't even cared whether they were guilty or innocent.

I would take this burden from you if I could, child, E.Z. said. *But too much depends on the success of your mission.*

"I can't do this by myself!"

Your uncertainty diminishes us both. You are a Windsinger, you grow more powerful with every passing day. Never doubt this. And I will be with you, as much as I am able.

"Will I ever see you again?"

All things are possible, child.

A knock sounded on her door. She felt the presence vanish but had no doubt it would be back.

"Come in," she called, turning to face the door.

Vida stood on the threshold holding a bundle in her arms. For a moment the two women simply looked at each other, taking each other's measure.

"I thought you might appreciate a change of clothing," Vida said. "It's probably going to be a little big on you, but it's the best I could do for now."

"You're very kind," Nakeisha said, taking the bundle.

"If you're feeling up to it, the captain would like to speak with you."

"I understand. I am sure he has many questions." She noted the other woman's hesitation. "If you care to wait until I've changed my clothing, I will accompany you to the captain."

Vida gave her a faint smile and came in to wait.

Chapter Three

"We've got a problem," Blake said to Chaney. They were alone in the lounge, a perfect opportunity for a private chat.

Chaney raised an eyebrow. "Just one?" So far this trip had been nothing but problems.

"We have a leak," the captain said grimly. He paced over to the observation port and then turned to face Chaney again.

"I take it we're not talking about a leak in a fuel or coolant line?"

"I've thought so for some time now. We've had too many close calls with both Corporate and Sector for it to be mere coincidence."

Chaney grimaced. You'd think after the seven year war with the Kohl-trin that the beings of the universe would crave peace. But no, instead the civilizations that had allied under the Pan-Galactic Council's banner had fractured into a myriad of warring factions, the two most powerful being the Corporate Alliance and the Sector Federation. "You think they're working together on this?" That would be bad, very bad. Not only for them, but for the whole quadrant.

"I can't shake the feeling that something's not right . . . I think this whole thing is much bigger than we've been led to believe."

"Why are you telling me this? Aren't I as much a suspect as everyone else?"

"You're about the only one I can trust," Blake replied. "Loyalty is hardwired into your genetic makeup."

It wasn't quite that simple, but few outsiders knew of the Paf D'Uron, the seven ordeals that turned a tribesman into a Fedylian. The process was not to be undertaken lightly and many did not survive. But those that did were gifted with unwavering loyalty to a cause, once their word was given. Chaney hadn't realized the captain knew his tribal rank. "So what do we do now?"

Blake sighed. "I don't know. Just be extra careful, and extra vigilant. Keep your eyes open."

"Aye, aye, sir," Chaney said. "Should I call Nigel and Libby to join us?"

Blake shook his head. "No, I think the three of us will be enough. I don't want our guest to feel too over-whelmed."

"So what have you decided to do about her?" Chaney asked.

"If I didn't know better, I'd say that was a show of curiosity. Better watch it, Chaney, you might start turning human on us."

The younger man scowled in mock anger. "I am human. I just don't see the need to be so blatant about it."

Blake laughed. "In answer to your question, we really don't have much choice, we'll have to take her with us for now, but no one is to mention our mission. As far as she's concerned we're just traders."

The door slid open again to admit Vida and Nakeisha.

Chaney straightened against the wall he'd been leaning casually on. Cleaned up and dressed in one of Vida's flowing, white pajama suits, Nakeisha was even more waif-like in appearance. She looked like a child who'd borrowed her big sister's clothes to play dress up in, although there was nothing childish about the curves beneath the flowing white.

Their eyes met, then hers flicked towards the bandage still on his hand and a slight flush suffused his face before she gave a faint nod. Chaney felt a moment of confusion at his reaction. He had no reason to feel shame at the sight of the mark on that delicate skin, but he did, despite the fact that her nod had been one of acknowledgment, warrior to warrior.

"If you'd all take a seat," the captain said, "we have a few things to discuss."

Nakeisha took a moment to study the people in the room with her. They were human in appearance, though just how human remained to be seen. Without realizing it, her eyes lingered longest on the warrior, Chaney. There was something about him . . . She would do well to stay on her guard.

The captain waited until everyone was comfortable before beginning. "We owe you a debt of gratitude," he said to Nakeisha.

This was so unexpected she was unable to hide her surprise.

"Our trade negotiations with the T'tenet were not going well," he continued. "If it hadn't been for your distraction Chaney and I might not have escaped."

"It is well that my impulsiveness had some merit to it," she said cautiously. "I hasten to assure you it is not in my nature to be so . . . volatile."

"We understand," Vida assured her. "There were . . . extenuating circumstances."

Nakeisha looked from one sympathetic face to another. "The doctor's scan revealed I had been tortured," she said bluntly.

"I'm sorry," Blake said sincerely. "But we need—"

"You need to know why," she finished for him. "This isn't just morbid curiosity . . ."

"I understand, Captain. We are strangers, thrown together by circumstance." She sighed and shifted in her seat. "My companion and I are . . . scholars on a pilgrimage. We were making our way to Kendra when the T'tenet captured us."

"Companion?" Vida asked in dismay. "You mean we left someone behind?"

"No, I—I apologize for my phrasing. My companion is no more."

"What would the T'tenet want with a pair of scholars?" Chaney asked. It didn't make any sense. He had a gut feeling there was more to her story, just as something told him there was much more to her as well. Her voice was mesmerizing, he had to force himself to concentrate on what she was saying.

"I do not know," Nakeisha said softly. "They were seeking information we could not give them."

Could not, or would not, Chaney wondered. What courage it must have taken to resist. Despite his misgivings his admiration for this woman continued to grow.

"Perhaps it was a case of mistaken identity," she continued. "Whatever the reason, my companion died to give me the chance to escape."

"And so you have," Vida said. "As you said, we've been brought together by circumstance and coincidence."

Nakeisha had no answer for that other than to wonder if it really had been coincidence that brought them together on Temus, or if there was something else at work.

"Kendra is a little out of our way," Captain Blake said abruptly, coming to a decision. The T'tenet seldom left their own system so they were unlikely to pursue the Comet. "Our next port of call is Tersic – you should be able to find passage from there."

"Passage to Tersic would suit me well," she said gravely, careful to let none of her relief show. "I have . . . friends on Tersic." At least she hoped they were friends.

"In that case, let me be the first to welcome you aboard the Burning Comet," Blake said.

Nakeisha kept to herself, for the most part, during the journey to Tersic. A part of her craved human companionship, the face of the one called Chaney flashed through her mind, but another part of her did not want these people embroiled in her difficulties. She'd already caused enough trouble for them and despite the captain's reassurances to the contrary, she felt guilty over the death of the crewman on Temus.

She did not for a moment believe they were a trading vessel – a ship this size should have far more crew, and where was their cargo, and guards? No, something else was going on, but as long as they took her to Tersic she was just as happy not knowing.

On the second day of her self-imposed exile, her meditation was interrupted by a knock on the door. She opened it to find the doctor, Nigel, holding a flower.

"If we were at a spaceport I could give you a bouquet of real flowers," he said, holding the bloom out to her, "But since we're not, this will have to do."

Standing aside to let him enter, she accepted the flower. Holding it to her nose she inhaled its spicy aroma. "It's very unusual. What is it?"

"Since we're short-handed we've been doubling up on duties and I was lucky enough to draw the hydroponics bay. It's an agrae blossom, an interesting addition to any salad. If you're hungry later you can use it for a snack," he said with a grin.

She returned his smile and sniffed the flower again before filling a glass with water to set it in.

"I thought you might be getting a little bored," he continued, "and as your doctor I'd advise strongly against that."

"And what do you advise to combat boredom?"

"I'd advise a tour of the ship," he said. "With yours truly as your guide of course."

"Of course," she echoed.

It was nothing she could put her finger on, but there was something about the doctor that was a little off. He was just a little too friendly, a little too eager to please. Maybe it was just that it had been a while since she'd been around humans.

Nakeisha hesitated.

Oh, why not? E.Z. whispered in her mind. *You have a handsome young man dancing attendance on you and I'm as interested in seeing the rest of the ship as you are.*

I wish you'd stop doing that, she thought back at him, her face giving nothing away of her inner turmoil. *It is most disconcerting.*

What's even more disconcerting is your longing for others of your own kind and your refusal to acknowledge it.

She turned her snort into a cough when Nigel gave her a concerned look.

"Perhaps you would rather I came back at another time?"

"I'm sorry," she said, laying a hand on his arm. "My thoughts were elsewhere for a moment. I would be happy to have you give me a tour of the ship."

He grinned down at her and tucked her hand beneath his arm, leading her towards the door. "Then why don't we start with hydroponics and I can impress you with my skills as a gardener."

Nigel was both a charming and entertaining tour guide, and after an hour in his company Nakeisha found it easy to forget why she was on board the ship in the first place.

"You have a great many empty berths," she commented as they wandered through the lower decks. "How large is the crew?"

"The Comet can accommodate a crew of thirty. We usually keep it to around half of that. Unfortunately, we've run into some bad luck this trip and it's down to just the five of us."

"And are you all from the same world?" she asked, genuinely curious.

Nigel laughed, a not altogether pleasant sound. "Not even close. Captain Blake and I come from Colora Prime. Vida is Uprien and Libby is from Bediali."

She nodded. "I have heard of Bediali. It is well known for its hospitality, and its people for their great beauty. I fear I know nothing of Uprien."

"It's not surprising. Uprien is on the far edge of the galaxy. It's as cold and inhospitable as its people."

Was that a thread of bitterness in his tone? Nakeisha hid her surprise. Vida had seemed neither cold nor inhospitable. Perhaps there were some ill feelings between the doctor and the second in command.

"And what of the navigator, Chaney?" Though she kept her voice casual, her pulse rate sped up slightly.

Nigel shot her a look. "The man who attacked you? He's from Soropo," he said, as though that explained everything.

This time Nakeisha let her surprise show. "What is a desert tribesman doing in space?"

The doctor shrugged. "Who knows?" he countered. "He's been with Captain Blake for years; I've only been part of the crew for the last two."

They bypassed the empty cargo bay and meandered back up to the main part of the ship.

"What is this?" she asked as they approached a plain, white door.

"This is probably the least used room in the ship," he told her, as the door slid open. "I've found my duties keep me in good enough shape that I don't really need to work out much."

"Which is why you're so soft," said a voice from inside.

Nakeisha quickly smothered her grin as a look of annoyance flashed across Nigel's face. "I'm sorry, I didn't know anyone was here. We can come back another time."

"It's no bother," Chaney said. "I was just about done anyway." He disengaged himself from the machine he was working on and stood up, draping a towel around his neck.

A shiver went through Nakeisha. The navigator was dressed only in a pair of tight, black shorts and his dark hair was pulled back off his face and confined in a tail. The muscles rippling under the sun bronzed skin glistened with sweat. It was obvious that he made very good use of the work-out room.

"I should probably get you back to your room," Nigel said, pulling her, none too gently, towards the door. "I've been enjoying myself so much in your company I forget that you're still recovering from your ordeal on Temus. You should get some rest."

She went without protest, a fact Chaney was quick to note. It made no difference to him who she chose to spend time with. She'd be gone soon anyway. He stared moodily at the punching bag and then lashed out with a series of lightning fast strikes. It made no difference at all.

Chapter Four

"You wanted to see me, Cap?" Chaney poked his head inside the door to the captain's cabin.

"Come in and sit down." The captain looked grave. "I've just received a coded message from the council—"

"Coded?"

"Coded," Blake confirmed. "We have new orders that supersede our previous ones."

Chaney frowned. "It's not like the council hasn't done that to us before, several times as a matter of fact."

"This is different. They want us to stop the search. We've been given a new mission."

"But we're so close!"

"I know, I tried to tell them, but I was told the search wouldn't be necessary if we succeed with this mission."

Chaney opened his mouth and then snapped it shut again. It was not his place to question orders, especially orders that came straight from the council. It just confirmed the belief that this whole thing was bigger than they'd been led to believe.

"Did you tell them your suspicions about information being leaked?"

"Yes, and they weren't surprised in the least."

Though Blake could understand the need for secrecy, he did not enjoy feeling like he was being deliberately kept out of the loop. Their primary mission had been to search for the location of one of the mythic worlds. With the galaxy fragmented in the aftermath of the war, the Council felt it was imperative to bring as many of the so called mythic worlds of the Old Races under their protection as possible.

"I don't suppose they offered any suggestions on how to ferret out the traitor?"

The captain snorted. "What do you think? All they said was to be extra careful."

"And so of course they turn around and give us a new mission, like that's not going to arouse any suspicions."

"Actually, it might not. Not if this is handled right. I have a plan," the captain said with a glint in his eye.

"Why do I get the feeling this plan of yours doesn't bode well for me?" Chaney got up and went over to the bar nestled in a corner of the cabin. Helping himself he held up a bottle and asked, "Drink?"

"Since it's my whiskey, yes."

He poured another, delivering it to the captain on his way back to his seat.

"So, if we're not going to pursue any leads on Tersic, where are we headed?"

"That's the strange part, our destination is still the Great Library. Only we're not going for research, we're going to pick something up."

"They want to use the Burning Comet as a courier ship?" Chaney asked in disgust. He took a large sip of his drink.

"My contact was rather pleased we were already headed there. I gather he'd been trying to make contact for several days to divert us. Whatever we're picking up, it's crucial it gets safely to the council."

"Which means they need to sneak it in, instead of using regular channels." Chaney guessed.

"So it would seem."

"Am I to assume you don't want the others knowing yet?"

"As far as they're concerned, we're just making our scheduled stop on Tersic."

The young navigator made the next logical leap. "So this plan of yours involves me getting the package on board without anyone else knowing because you don't know who might leak the information to the wrong person."

The captain beamed at him. "I knew you'd be happy to volunteer for the job."

"Happy isn't exactly the word I'd have chosen." Chaney polished off his drink.

"Does this plan of yours include any details of how I'm to accomplish this?"

"As a matter of fact . . ."

"Figures," Chaney muttered.

"Once we land you'll escort Nakeisha off the ship, for her own protection naturally–"

"Naturally."

"–and once you've seen her safely to her friends you'll make straight for the Great Library to make contact. One of the sub-librarians will be waiting for you."

"Any idea what this package is? How big it is?"

"Not a clue."

"What happens if it's too big to smuggle onto the ship without anyone else seeing it?"

"Then you contact me and I'll think of something to occupy everyone with."

Chaney went back to the bar and poured himself another drink. This is the kind of thing that drew him to space in the first place, the unknown. Who knew what might be laying in wait for him at the Library? It was that thrill of the unknown that sent a frisson of anticipation through him.

As an added bonus, he'd get some alone time with Nakeisha. Maybe once this was all over and everything was settled down again he could look her up. There was more to her than met the eye and he'd love nothing more than to get to the bottom of her particular mystery.

"So," he said, turning back to the captain. "How soon do we reach Tersic?"

"Is the world you come from like this?" Nakeisha asked, as she and Chaney made their way through the city.

The ship had landed without further incident on Tersic and after saying her goodbyes to the crew there seemed to be no reason to linger.

"It's true I come from a desert world," Chaney replied, "And there are some similarities, but Soropo is much . . ." he glanced around with a grimace, "cleaner."

Tersic was hot, arid and dusty. Even without a wind to blow it around, the reddish grey grit seemed to cover everything.

"You need not stay," Nakeisha said, once they reached the library. It was an imposing structure built entirely out of red stone. "I am sure my friends will be here momentarily."

She had no idea what kind of arrangements E.Z. had made, but she was sure that Chaney was not a part of them.

"I don't mind waiting," Chaney said easily. "Besides, I might never get another chance to have a look inside the Great Library. This is the stuff of legends."

The man who greeted them frowned slightly at Chaney's weapon, but did not request that he remove it. They were led to a reception room and told to wait.

At one time Tersic had been considered the center of the galaxy. That, along with the fact that it had little to do with galactic politics, made it the logical choice when the library was first constructed. When the seat of power shifted, the library had already grown to such enormous proportions there seemed no point in trying to move it as well.

Chaney just hoped that whoever his contact was waited until Nakeisha was gone before giving him the package. Nakeisha appeared to have enough problems of her own, she didn't need to get caught up in council conspiracies too. He had to admit that he was sorry they'd be parting company. Nakeisha was an intriguing woman – there was something about her that drew him like no one had ever done before.

They did not have long to wait. Moments later the door opened for one of the under librarians. The man's eyes widened. His stoic expression was replaced by astonishment and a trace of fear when he spied Nakeisha.

"Forgive me," he gasped, dropping to the floor. "They did not tell me you were *Illarie*."

"*Hydami*," Nakeisha snapped. "Be at ease. I believe I am expected."

The man straightened up, although he kept his head bowed. "This way, *Illarie*." Without giving her a chance to say anything to Chaney, he guided her out of the room.

It happened so quickly that Chaney was caught by surprise. He stared after them, freezing for a few seconds and then vaulted out of his chair. As fast as he was, by the time he reached the corridor they were gone. He grabbed one of the passing workers by the arm.

"Two people were just out here, a man and a woman, which way did they go?"

The man gently disengaged himself. "If you would be so kind as to wait in the reception room, someone will be with you in a moment sir."

For a moment Chaney thought about arguing with him then realized there would be no point. Nakeisha was gone and that was that. She had her life to go back to and he had a mission. It's not like there was anything between them, although it would have been nice to have at least said goodbye.

With a last look down the corridor, he returned to the waiting room. Restless, he paced back and forth. It was a good half hour before the door opened again. During that time Chaney thought of Nakeisha, and of the missed opportunities with Nakeisha. Like most of his people, he was fatalistic, if it was meant to be they would meet again. And he promised himself if they met again he would not waste any more opportunities.

It was an older gentleman who entered the room. "You are the representative from the Burning Comet?"

"Yes. I believe you have something for me?"

"It is being prepared," the man told him. "I cannot stress deeply enough that it is imperative that the Ardraci be delivered safely to the council."

Before Chaney could reply a series of explosions rocked the building. The old man was knocked to the floor. Chaney dodged a piece of collapsing ceiling as he moved to help him.

"We must pray it is not too late," the old man gasped. There was a trickle of blood on his forehead.

"You need to sit down," Chaney replied. "I'll go see–"

"You don't understand!" the old man grasped his arm. "There's no time! We've been betrayed. You must get the Ardraci to safety! Come with me, hurry!"

The corridor was chaos, students and scholars streaming by in panic. The old man was stronger than he looked, forcing himself against the flow, Chaney close on his heels. They went deeper into the library, passing fewer people.

At another time Chaney might have admired the frescoes and tapestries lining the walls as they passed into what was obviously a very ancient part of the library, but he'd caught the old man's sense of urgency and barely noticed them. Was it Sector or Corporate that was attacking the library, or was it a new faction altogether?

And what about Nakeisha? Had she and her friends made it out safely? Or had she been trapped? He paused when he heard shots but the old man urged him onwards.

"It is you and the Ardraci they seek. You must hide!" The old man pushed aside a tapestry and triggered a hidden mechanism that opened a door. "In here. You must stay here until it is safe."

With that he gave Chaney a shove that sent him careening into the room beyond and then closed the door behind him. Chaney yelled, pounding on the wall where he believed the door to be, but he could find no way out. A final strike against the wall and he gave up in disgust.

He activated the communicator on his wrist and was unsurprised when there was no response. The signal was being jammed. Furious, he paced the length of the room. It was long and narrow, dimly lit, with statues lining the length. There were benches between the statues and judging by the dust and cobwebs, the room had not been used in a very long time.

Unholstering his weapon he aimed at one of the walls, but hesitated before firing. The architecture of the room was old, but sturdy. His laser would have little effect on stone and he couldn't be sure of what was behind it. With a curse he sheathed his weapon again. It looked like he was effectively trapped, for now.

Chapter Five

Nakeisha was taken totally by surprise at how quickly she was separated from Chaney. She tried to tug herself free to say goodbye, but was pulled relentlessly away.

"What is the matter with you?" she demanded. "First you –"

"Forgive me, *Illarie*," the under-librarian said. "But we must hurry. Arrangements have been made for you to continue your journey."

After one fleeting glance backwards, Nakeisha swallowed her protest and allowed herself to be rushed along the corridor. It's not like she really had anything to say to Chaney, goodbyes were always awkward. But there was a part of her that would always regret that she never had a chance to get to know him better.

She lost count of the twists and turns they took. If she were separated from her guide she'd never find her way out again. At last they stopped in front of a carved door in an older section of the library.

"There is clothing and refreshment awaiting you," the under-librarian told her. "The Master Librarian will be with you momentarily. If you have need of anything, there is a summoning bell."

He was gone before she could thank him. Nakeisha shrugged and went into the room. It was much like the room she and Chaney had been waiting in, save for the tray of food sitting on the table and the wardrobe in the corner.

She wandered over to the tray, but didn't feel particularly hungry. The thought of what may lay ahead killed her appetite. With a sigh she crossed to the wardrobe and opened the doors. A faint smile crossed her face. Most of the clothing was in pale shades of silver grey, flowing robes and tunics with matching trousers.

I'd choose something in a dark color, E.Z.'s voice whispered in her mind. *Preferably something you can fight in.*

"Are you expecting trouble?" Nakeisha asked, a frown creasing her brow.

Most certainly.

A shelf in the top of the wardrobe held darker clothes of a strong but supple material more to her liking. Nakeisha changed into a form-fitting outfit and just finished braiding her hair when there was a knock on the door.

The Master Librarian bowed low. "May the Winds seek only the truth, the Fires burn bright, the Earth be free, and the Water be pure."

"And may all who believe be blessed," Nakeisha answered. "I–"

A sudden explosion shook the room. Wide-eyed, she took a step forward and had to hang on to the edge of the table to keep from being knocked down as a series of explosions followed.

"They dare to attack the Library?" The Master Librarian was more angry than frightened.

"Who–"

Another explosion rocked the room causing tiles to fall from the ceiling. The Master Librarian took her by the arm and pulled her out of the room, stooping to collect a pack that was resting against the wall by the door. "Come," he said. "It is not safe to stay here."

More explosions shook the building as they made their way deeper inside the labyrinthine library. At one point Nakeisha was sure she heard shots being fired. The Great Library was an honored seat of knowledge that had stood for centuries, she felt sick at the damage being done.

"Here," he said, stopping suddenly. "There is a room within. You will be safe in the sanctuary."

"What about you?" Nakeisha asked.

"My duty is to the Library," he said with dignity. He handed her the pack. "Most of your things were sent ahead to the transport. This was prepared ahead of time in case of trouble. I will send someone to you when it is safe to return to the spaceport."

He fit his fingers into the filigree of one of the frescoes on the wall and there was a grinding noise as one of the panels slid to the side. Nakeisha stared down into the dark, narrow passage.

"The Library was built around an ancient temple that is filled with secret passages. Once you are at the end of the tunnel there is a lever you must pull to access the sanctuary. It saved the lives of many priests during the Holy Wars."

Another explosion shook the building.

"Hurry!" he urged. "You will be safe inside."

"Thank you," Nakeisha said. "This will not be forgotten."

She ducked down into the passage. As soon as she was clear of the entrance the Master Librarian closed it behind her. There was a momentary flash of claustrophobia but she shook it off. She could not afford to let fear get the better of her.

The passage was longer than she expected and there was no light, forcing her to move slowly. She felt her way carefully, smooth stone floor beneath her, rougher stone on either side, the occasional cobweb startling her as it brushed her face. Finally she reached what she perceived to be the end. Feeling around on the wall in front of her, she found the lever and pulled it. There was another grinding noise as something moved out of the way.

Chaney had no concept of the passage of time, though he knew it was probably less time than he thought. He started pacing up and down in the narrow room. A sudden noise, from near one of the statues had him whirling around, flattening himself to the wall beside the statue.

The statue began to move, revealing a low opening behind it. What looked like a pack was tossed through the opening, followed by a slight, black-clad figure. As the statue began to move back into place, Chaney grabbed the intruder and yanked him upright, arm across his throat. The figure froze with a gasp.

Chaney froze momentarily as well. He recognized that gasp. Before he knew what he was doing, he shifted his grip on his prisoner and brought his lips down hard on hers.

The kiss was over before she had a chance to struggle and he released her quickly. "I'm sorry, I shouldn't—"

"Chaney! You're here!" Nakeisha hugged him closer until the sound of another explosion broke them apart.

"I thought I'd never see you again!"

"I was worried about you!"

They spoke at the same time. Nakeisha looked away first, a faint flush suffusing her face as she loosened her hold on him.

"What are you still doing here?" Chaney asked. He refused to apologize for the kiss. "Where are your friends? Were they caught in the blast?"

Trying to gather her scattered thoughts, she paced to the other side of the narrow room. She was glad he was here with her, though she really hadn't expected to see him again. How much should she tell him?

"The Master Librarian brought me here to protect me from the bombing," she answered. "Who would do such a thing? To attack the Great Library . . ." She sank down to a seat on one of the benches.

"I don't know," he said truthfully. He crouched down to examine the opening she'd entered through. It had closed behind her and wouldn't budge. "The under-librarian hustled me in here before I could find out what's going on."

He straightened up and then joined her on the bench. Another series of blasts could be heard faintly and the room trembled around them. Chaney put his arm around her, for comfort, and Nakeisha leaned against him.

"I admit I am glad to not be alone," she said, though she found it very strange that they were hidden in the same place.

Perhaps it's not just a coincidence, E.Z. whispered in her mind.

"I have little patience when it comes to waiting," Chaney admitted. "But your presence here helps."

"Why are you here?" Nakeisha asked suddenly. "I would have thought you'd be back at the ship by now."

It was his turn for discomfort. "I—" he hesitated, torn between the truth and a lie. "I had ship's business to attend to," he finished lamely. Let her make of that what she would.

E.Z.? she asked in her mind. Of course E.Z. was silent again. Perhaps he already knew the conclusion she'd come to. She smiled faintly.

"Then it seems our paths were not yet meant to part."

They sat in companionable silence for a time, listening to the vague sounds of the explosions outside the sanctuary. It didn't take long for Chaney to become restless again and he began to pace the confines of the room. At last he stopped in front of one of the statues.

"Where do you think these statues came from?" he asked.

Nakeisha joined him in front of the white marble figure of a youth holding out his hands, eyes raised in supplication. There was writing on the base and she stooped to read.

"This statue is The Quest for Knowledge, and dedicated to Rumplari, First Priest of the Realm. The Great Library was originally a temple. The Master Librarian told me this was a sanctuary where priests were hidden during the Holy Wars."

"The Holy Wars? They were centuries ago!"

She nodded. "And in all that time this building has stood untouched."

"Until now."

"Until now," she agreed.

"What could be so important as to risk the wrath of the Pan-Galactic Council by attacking the Library?"

"I–" Nakeisha hesitated, on the verge of telling him the truth.

There was a scraping sound and the panel Chaney entered by opened. A young man, dressed in the robes of a library technician, slipped into the chamber. He moved with sharp, jerky motions, eyes darting around the room before settling on the couple standing between the statues.

"Dress in robes," he said in broken Standard, thrusting a bundle towards them. "You leave now."

"Is it safe? Has the attack stopped? Do they know who was attacking in the first place?"

The young man backed away from Chaney's rapid fire questions. "Dress in robes," he repeated, a little desperately.

Nakeisha took the bundle from him. There were two nondescript robes, such as might be worn by one of the townsfolk, complete with head wrappings. She slipped the smaller robe over her head and then handed the other to Chaney.

"This might be our only chance to leave," she said. "I think we should take it."

He opened his mouth, then shut it again and took the robe from her. As much as he hated to leave his questions unanswered, she was probably right. It was still a long way from the library to the space port.

As he dressed she checked the contents of her pack, withdrawing a small bundle of currency and packet of identification papers that she concealed inside her clothing. Unfortunately, there were no weapons.

Once they were both dressed the technician led them out of the sanctuary. The corridor was rubble strewn and cloudy with dust. They met not a single soul as they wound their way through the maze of passageways, the damage increasing the closer they came to the main entrance.

Nakeisha stopped before they actually entered the great hall. "Are you sure it's safe to leave this way?"

Chaney had been having doubts since the panel opened. The robes the so-called technician was wearing did not fit him properly and he was too nervous. Was he even really a library technician? Although he could no longer hear the sound of explosions, he was sure he heard the whine of laser fire.

"You go," their guide insisted. Though pale, there was a sheen of sweat on his face. "Back to ship." He turned and fled, gone before they had a chance to question him further.

"What now?" Nakeisha asked.

There was a grim look on Chaney's face as he watched their guide disappear. He tried the communicator again but it was still being jammed. Turning his attention back to her, he felt more confused than ever at the turn of events. "We don't have much choice. Either lose ourselves back in the maze, or some how make our way to the ship."

Chapter Six

Nakeisha sighed, not liking either of the choices before them. They could turn back the way they'd come and hope to either find the sanctuary again or some other hiding place, or they could take their chances with the unknown enemy that seemed bent on destroying the library.

You must leave now, E.Z. said, *before the fighting spreads to the space port.*

"How far do you think it is to the space port?" Nakeisha asked. "I confess I was not paying close attention once we found transportation." It seemed so long ago now, and her mind had been on what lay ahead.

"I wasn't paying attention either," Chaney admitted. He had been focused on the woman beside him in the ground car. "But I believe I could find the way.

I'll leave the choice of whether we try or not up to you."

You can trust the tribesman, E.Z. whispered.

What's that supposed to mean? she thought back. *How far do I trust him?*

He will not lead you false.

Nakeisha waited for E.Z. to say more, but his presence was gone again.

"All right," she said. "We've come this far, we might as well make a run for it."

The approval in Chaney's eyes made her glad of her choice. She found it much easier to be brave when she didn't feel so alone.

Never alone, E.Z. whispered.

Chaney drew closer then gathered her in his arms. It might be a long time before he had another chance like this. Being of a practical nature, he decided to take it.

"For luck," he said, and then kissed her. It was a gentle brush of the lips that was more of a promise than anything else.

Nakeisha felt an unaccustomed warmth suffuse her. Of their own accord, her hands crept up to thread through his hair and she kissed him back. Blushing, she released him and took a step back.

"For luck," she said, unable to meet his eye. What was wrong with her? She had never been so bold with a man before. And these were hardly the circumstances to start.

He grinned and took her hand, lacing his fingers through hers. Cautiously, they approached the door. The Great Hall of the library appeared empty, but Chaney paused just inside the door and then quickly pulled her into the shadow of one of the massive columns surrounding the hall.

"What's the matter," Nakeisha whispered.

"There's something not right about this."

She cocked her head to listen, then shrugged. "I don't . . ."

Concentrate, E.Z. whispered.

Taking a deep breath she cleared her mind and tried again. A light breeze stirred up the dust in the room. She could hear it now, the faint sound of lasers, either much deeper in the library or somewhere in the city. There was also the sound of someone nearby moving restlessly. Maybe even several someones.

"We're not alone, are we?" she asked softly.

"It's too quiet. I don't like it." Chaney was a man used to trusting his gut instincts and his gut was telling him they were walking into a trap. He studied the room, mentally checking for hiding places.

"You don't think that technician . . ."

He shot her a quick glance and went back to scanning the room. "That's just what I was thinking. I should have known better."

Nakeisha touched his arm. "You could not have known. Our safety was compromised the moment he opened the panel."

"Thank you," he brought her hand up and brushed a kiss against her knuckles. "But I still allowed us to follow him like *chellas* to a butcher."

She opened her mouth to argue that no one allowed her to do anything, then shut it again as E.Z.s voice whispered through her mind.

You would do well to practice your diplomacy, he said. *It is his nature to be protective.*

"What do you suggest we do?" she asked aloud.

Chaney sighed. "We really don't have much choice but to go forward. We'll just need to be very careful."

The sun was beginning to set, taking the natural light with it, and the shadows in the hall were lengthening. As quietly as possible they circled around towards the main entrance, keeping to the edge of the room. They were about halfway to the door when they were discovered.

"Crap," Chaney said succinctly.

There were five of them, dressed in nondescript black uniforms. Chaney used his hand to gently push Nakeisha behind him.

"I want you to stay behind this pillar," he said.

When she would have protested he cut her off. "I know you're a capable fighter, but I'm armed and you're not."

Her mouth closed with a snap and she gave him a sharp nod of acknowledgment. Independent she may be, but she wasn't going to be stupid about it. A breeze snaked its way into the entrance hall, stirring up the dust. The wind began to pick up outside the library.

"I'll try to draw their fire and when I do I want you to make for the door."

"But—"

"Trust me, it's our best chance."

He didn't give her another opportunity to argue. The five men had fanned out. Chaney chose his target and then fired, ducking back behind the pillar as the man collapsed with a yell and his companions returned fire.

"Get ready," he told Nakeisha.

He let off a series of shots from his blaster and raced for cover, heading back the way they'd come. Nakeisha waited a heartbeat to make sure their attention was on Chaney before making her own move. Staying as deep in the shadows as she could, she continued circling towards the main entrance.

She plastered herself against the back of the next pillar as someone fired at her. This set off another flurry of shots as Chaney continued in the opposite direction to draw their fire.

"I want them alive!" someone bellowed from the shadows.

Nakeisha shouted a warning, but it was too late as three more men came up behind Chaney. She couldn't help but be impressed at the way he fought them off. Even after they managed to disarm him he was still a deadly fighter.

Another of them reached the pillar sheltering Nakeisha. When he saw her slight form he grinned and holstered his weapon. That was his first mistake, the only one he had time for before Nakeisha went on the offensive.

She fought with a strength and skill that belied her size. The man who came after her was quickly dispatched, as was the one who came after him. She may not have had a blaster, but she was far from defenseless.

Chaney began to work his way back towards her. He recalled the streets of the city as being narrow and twisting. If they could make it to the outside they might have a chance of getting to the space port.

"Surrender and you won't be harmed," the mysterious voice called out.

His words seemed to infuriate Nakeisha. She let loose with a string of words Chaney was unable to interpret and followed them with a flurry of movement, attacking the three men left surrounding her. Chaney had only a brief moment to admire her fighting skill before more men poured into the room from the library.

"Come, on," he yelled, reaching her side.

With a spinning kick to the mid-section of the last man near her, she turned her attention to Chaney and caught herself before attacking him as well.

"Let's go," he said, holding out his hand.

She hesitated only a fraction of a second before taking his hand. Together, they sprinted for the entrance of the library. Someone fired a laser after them, but missed, gouging a large chunk out of the door.

"I thought they wanted us alive," Nakeisha gasped.

"I guess they'd rather see us dead than take a chance on losing us altogether." Chaney answered.

They fled down the library stairs and into the wind storm that was building up outside.

"Which way?" Nakeisha yelled over the sound of the wind.

"This way," Chaney said decisively.

Holding a fold of their robes across their faces to combat the dust, they raced straight across the piazza in front of the library. The men following them dropped back slightly in the face of the dust laden wind. Once across the piazza they were somewhat sheltered, but the wind still blew past them in gusts, stirring up clouds of dust in its wake. Chaney tried his communicator again but it was still being jammed.

He guided Nakeisha down a side street, following it for several yards before turning onto another. They raced past countless shops and homes, closed up tight against the wind storm. Two more turns and then he pulled her into the relative cover of a doorway so they could catch their breath, placing her with her back to the door and sheltering her from the worst of the wind with his body.

He leaned closer to her ear. "I think we may have lost them, but I want to keep going while we still have the cover of the dust storm."

"I do not believe they will be too far behind," she agreed. "And they must realize where we will be headed."

"My thoughts exactly," he said. "I – why are you smiling?"

Nakeisha's smile broadened. "You are covered in red dust," she replied. "I would not have chosen it as your color, but it is quite fetching on you."

He grinned back at her. "You look quite becoming as a red head yourself. Are you ready to go?"

She nodded and they continued towards the space port.

Chapter Seven

The wind storm kept up a steady presence as they continued towards the space port. It always seemed worse behind them and before them, never so bad where they actually were. Chaney was just grateful they could see which way to go.

They passed no other people, not even so much as a ground car. As they neared their destination, he became more cautious, keeping watch for an ambush or trap. Their luck appeared to be holding but they hadn't made it this far trusting in luck. Just outside the space port he paused and pulled Nakeisha to a stop again.

"What's wrong?" she asked.

"This was too easy," he said, glancing around.

"You call this easy?" she stood slightly bent over, trying to control her breathing. "I feel like I've inhaled half the planet."

"I just can't shake the feeling . . ." his voice trailed off as he peered intently ahead of them.

"How much farther to the ship?"

"It's in slip seven-seven-three, in blue sector. We're at the edge of green sector, two more sections to go to reach blue."

Nakeisha looked around uneasily, Chaney's mood was infectious. The same dust storm that had seemed so helpful for their escape was now a hazard in reaching the ship. Anyone, or anything, could be hiding in the swirling clouds of red dust.

The wind died slightly, allowing glimpses of cargo on loading docks, supplies waiting to be loaded, and other vague shapes. Suddenly, Nakeisha wasn't liking the looks of what lay ahead either.

"We don't really have much choice, do we?" she asked.

"No," Chaney agreed. "Not really. Even if there was any place else for us to go, it would be closed because of the storm."

Her sigh was lost in the sound of the wind. "Do you think they will have someone waiting for us?"

He tried to smile down at her, but she wasn't fooled. "I don't know what to think," he said honestly. "But it seems like a logical move to me."

She laid one slender hand on his chest. "We will just have to be very careful then."

Chaney covered her hand with one of his own and gave it a soft squeeze. "We should keep to the loading docks as much as possible, it'll provide the most cover."

He let her lead the way as they slowly approached the space port and nodded when she looked back at him, a question in her eyes. The wind appeared to be losing strength. Using what cover there was, she moved to the first loading dock, Chaney following close behind.

In this manner they made it through the green section and were just approaching red when there was a burst of laser fire. They quickly ducked down behind a stack of metal boxes.

"Damn it, we were so close!" Chaney chastised himself mentally. This was just supposed to be a simple trip – escort Nakeisha to her friends and make a pick up at the library. He'd failed on both counts.

"They seem to be concentrated over there," Nakeisha said, pointing. "If we go that way, we should be able to circle around to the blue section."

"All right," he agreed. "Make for that opening and I'll be right behind you."

Staying in a crouch, she moved into position and waited. When there was a break in the shots being fired she bolted towards the next loading dock. There was a renewed flurry of fire right on her heels. Another pause and then Chaney joined her behind the barrels she'd taken shelter behind, seconds ahead of more laser fire.

"If they weren't shooting at us, I'd be impressed with their aim."

She shot him a look. "That was almost too close."

"Fortunately, almost doesn't count. Get ready, we need to keep our momentum."

Nodding, she got into position again. This time she waited until there was a gust of dust laden wind to protect her before scurrying to the next loading bay. Chaney was not so lucky. Halfway to where Nakeisha was concealed a stray blast caught him. He fell soundlessly.

"Chaney!"

Oblivious to both the storm and the laser fire, she raced back towards him. The wind picked up in a swirl of red dust as she knelt at his side.

"Chaney, tell me you're all right!"

"Go on without me. We're almost to the ship."

"No!"

"Go, get help."

"I will not leave you behind," she said fiercely.

He reached up and gently touched her face, leaving streaks like teardrops on her cheek before his hand fell away.

When Chaney came to he was lying on a hard surface but his head was cushioned by something soft. He was disoriented for a few seconds and then came fully awake with a shock.

"It's about time you awoke," Nakeisha said softly.

Apparently, she was the something soft his head was resting on, or more specifically, her lap.

"What—?"

"Easy," she helped him into a sitting position on the floor beside her.

"Where are we?"

The room they were in had a dirt floor, with walls made of local stone. There was a single light and a small window high above them, too small for anyone, even someone as small as Nakeisha, to fit through. There were no furnishings in the room, just a heavy, wooden door on the wall opposite them.

"We are in a store room of a home close to the space port," Nakeisha told him. "They brought us here directly from the space port."

They were no longer wearing the dust covered robes and there was a bandage on his side under his shirt.

"Who—"

"I demanded clean water and a cloth to treat your wound," she said grimly. "It was not as bad as I had feared. The laser cauterizes as it cuts. You lost some skin and some muscle, but nothing vital was touched."

"You should have escaped when you had the chance," he said, leaning his head back against the wall.

"Perhaps you should not have escorted me to the library," she retorted.

He turned his head to look at her.

She shrugged. "Who can say what small event triggers a larger one. All we can do is move forward from the moment we are at."

"Point taken," he said. "How long was I unconscious?"

"A few hours perhaps. I believe night has fallen."

"I don't suppose they said why they were shooting at us?"

Smiling faintly, she shook her head. "No, they did not speak to me at all. I believe they are some kind of mercenaries, doing someone else's biding. They seem to be waiting for orders of some kind."

"What kind of orders?" he wondered.

"That, I cannot tell you. It is just the impression they gave."

There was a rattle at their door. Nakeisha laid a restraining hand on Chaney's arm as he tensed. The door opened and while two men pointed lasers at them a third slide a tray inside the cell. Once he backed away, the other two left as well and the door clanked shut behind them.

Nakeisha got up and brought the tray over to where they were sitting.

"Do you think it's safe to eat any of this?"

"Probably. If they wanted us dead we'd have been dead by now, and if they wanted us unconscious they'd use the stun setting on their lasers. They don't seem the subtle type."

The meal consisted of fruit and hard, dry bread with a flask of water to wash it down with. Neither of them was very hungry and the food was not at all appetizing to them, but not knowing when their next meal might be they ate anyway.

After they were finished they sat side by side again. Nakeisha sighed and leaned her head against Chaney's good shoulder. He put his arm around her and held her close.

"Your friends will be wondering what happened to you," he said.

"I suspect they were among those who were killed in the Library."

"I wonder why the librarians chose to hide us together?"

"I am glad that they did," she said, raising her head to look at him. "I would not like to be here alone."

"It's my fault you're here," he said.

"Why would you think such a thing?"

"I insisted on accompanying you to the Library. If I hadn't, those raiders wouldn't have followed me and you wouldn't have been put in danger."

"Chaney, I don't think—"

"The Comet's been a target since before we picked you up on Temus. We've had trouble dogging our heels from the beginning."

"Chaney, you must listen to me—"

"Wait," he held up his hand for quiet. "Do you hear that?"

There was a sound beyond the door. Something was happening.

"Perhaps whoever is in charge has arrived. Chaney, before anything else happens, you must listen—"

A noise at the door effectively cut off what she was about to say. They tensed as the door swung open.

Chapter Eight

"Well," a familiar voice said. "Are you two going to just sit there or are you coming with us?"

"Vida?" Chaney asked in amazement.

"You don't look so good, Chaney," Vida said, poking her head around the door. "I suggest you two hurry up. Your guards won't stay unconscious forever."

Nakeisha helped Chaney to his feet. "How did you find us?"

"Libby and Nigel were in the market when the news of an attack on the Library swept through the crowd," Vida said, helping Nakeisha with Chaney when she realized he'd been injured. "We monitored the activity from the Comet – it seemed to be confined to the Library so we figured the best thing to do was wait."

The two guards were slumped next to the door, unconscious. Vida dragged them into the store room and closed the door.

"Just as the bombing, or whatever it was, died down, the wind picked up," she continued, "blowing that red grit around. It was almost impossible to see but Cap decided we couldn't wait any longer. We'd just left the ship when the fight broke out in the space port – it wasn't any surprise to see you in the thick of it."

They moved quickly down the hallway and out into the city. As Nakeisha had guessed, darkness had fallen, which was fortunate because the storm appeared to be over. They were joined by Cap who took over helping Chaney.

"No more talking until we're back at the ship. Nigel's led the rest away but they won't be gone for long."

Under the cover of night, they managed to get back to the ship without further incident. Nigel returned shortly after, pleased with himself for his part in the rescue. His cockiness turned to a frown when he realized Chaney had been hurt.

"It's astounding the way you seem to be able to draw trouble," he chided.

Ignoring Nigel, Blake said, "Now that we're all here together, maybe you'd like to share what happened."

"To be honest, Cap, I'm really not sure." Chaney leaned tiredly against the wall. "Nakeisha was to meet her friends at the Great Library so I escorted her there. I'm not familiar with Tersic so I wasn't sure if it was safe for a woman to travel alone."

"I'm with you so far," the captain said.

"While we were waiting inside the Library, it was attacked."

"That's the part I don't understand," Vida put in. "Who attacked the Library, and why?"

"We can only assume it was the same men who attacked us in the space port," Nakeisha said softly.

Nigel turned to Nakeisha and took her hand. "My dear, I am so happy to see you returned to us, and none the worse for wear."

Something seemed to tighten in Chaney's face as he watched Nigel. "Cap, might I suggest we take off before anything else happens?"

"That's probably a good idea," Blake said. "Vida, join Libby on the bridge, she's been keeping an eye on the sensors and I'll want a full report. Nigel, if you think you can tear yourself away, perhaps you could have a look at Chaney's wound, just to make sure he's all right."

When no one appeared inclined to move, he barked, "Move it!"

The crew scattered, leaving the captain and Nakeisha alone in the corridor. He looked at her with a frown. "I have a feeling you know a lot more about what's going on that you've been letting on."

She sighed wearily. "It's entirely possible, Captain. However, I do not believe it is wise to discuss it where we might be overheard."

"I agree. Perhaps we could meet in my cabin once we're under way." It sounded like more of an order than a request. "And if you don't mind I'd like Chaney to be present as well."

"That would be fine, Captain."

He took in her dust grimed appearance and his lips twitched trying to hold back a smile. "Maybe we should make that in two hours. It'll give you both a chance to clean up."

Visions of a hot bath filled her mind. It seemed like eons since she'd had a hot bath. Her eyes lit up. "Thank you, Captain."

"You can imagine my surprise when several boxes were delivered here for you," Blake continued, when she would have moved past him.

Nakeisha bit her lip. "I was told at the library that arrangements had made for me to continue my journey," she said carefully. "But they did not inform me what those arrangements were."

"I'm sure you'll understand my curiosity as to why they would choose the Comet, and just who "they" are for that matter."

"Captain, I—"

He held up a hand "You're right. This is not the place for this discussion. But I'm warning you right now – I *will* have my answers."

Nakeisha hesitated.

"I'd like to think we're on the same side," he said quietly.

"So would I, Captain. So would I."

"So," Nigel asked, a little too casually as he checked Chaney over. "What really happened in the library?"

Chaney frowned. "What do you mean?"

"You two were gone almost all day. The attack started just after mid-day."

"I didn't want to just leave her there, so I waited with her."

"How gallant of you," the doctor said with a slight sneer.

"It was just what I told the Captain. We went to the library, it was attacked, we escaped and made our way back to the space port. It took a little longer on foot."

"And you really have no idea who would attack the library?"

"Why would I? The attack came out of no where," Chaney replied. He'd been watching the doctor out of the corner of his eye and noted he seemed somewhat relieved by his answer.

"It just seems like an odd co-incidence," Nigel mused. "I wonder why Nakeisha came back here with you instead of leaving with her friends."

"I believe her friends were among those killed in the first wave of the attack," Chaney said quietly. "She didn't have any where else to go."

"Poor girl, I'll have to look in on her later." the doctor finished wrapping a clean bandage around Chaney's torso. "There, all finished. You'll want to go easy on the lifting or exercising for the next few days, but after that you should be all right."

"Thanks," Chaney said, jumping down off the examining table.

Though he couldn't have said why, there was something about the doctor that was giving him a twitchy feeling lately. Sighing, Chaney had to admit it was probably Nigel's attraction to Nakeisha. The good doctor had a definite way with women, one Chaney had never envied, until now.

He met Libby as he was making his way to his cabin to clean up and stopped her in the corridor.

"I have a favor to ask," he told her.

Libby raised a brow, the only sign of her surprise. Chaney was not normally one to ask favours.

"When I was in the Library, I heard a few words and I'm positive they were Ilezie. I was hoping you might know what they mean."

"I might," she said. "What were they?"

"One was *illarie*, one was *hydami*, and the last was *ardraci*."

"Let's see," Libby mused. She leaned back on the wall of the corridor, brow furrowed in concentration. "*Illarie* means vessel. *Hydami* is an order to be at ease, that formality is not necessary. *Ardraci* though, it might mean elemental, but I can't be sure."

"Vessel," he repeated. "A vessel for what, I wonder?"

"I can't tell you that without hearing the inflection." At his puzzled look she continued. "It can be a title or honorific, like you would give a priest or important person as a vessel of knowledge, or it could simply be a container that holds something of great value."

"Thank you," he said absently.

"No problem," Libby said, watching him continue down the corridor. It wasn't the first time a crew member had asked for an interpretation and she was sure it wouldn't be the last. Pushing off the wall she continued on her way.

Nakeisha let out a sigh and closed her eyes as she leaned back in the soapy water. Heaven, this was absolute heaven. The heat from the water relaxed her muscles and the aroma from the bath oil wafted upwards to relax her soul. Her worries were released with the steam, if only for a little while.

She could scarcely believe someone had the audacity to attack the Great Library of Temus. The big question, of course, was why. The information of the Great Library was free to all. The Librarians existed solely to aid seekers of knowledge and to accumulate more knowledge.

Which meant, of course, the attack was not meant for the library itself, but for someone within the library. The question remained, who were they after, her or Chaney? They both had their secrets it seemed. She had thought there was more to the Comet than there appeared to be, but she had also thought she'd only be here a short while. Now, however, everything had changed. She and the crew of the Comet seemed to be on a similar, if not the same, path. It was up to fate to see where that path led.

A slight smile crossed her face as she remembered the way fate had brought her and Chaney together again. He was every bit the warrior he appeared to be, but there was a great depth to him as well. She looked forward to getting to know the man as well as the warrior.

You took a great risk. E.Z.'s voice intruded on her serenity.

Though she kept her eyes closed, her muscles tensed. "To what are you referring?"

You should have left him behind.

"Like I did you?"

Yes.

"No." She opened her eyes. All pretense of relaxing gone. "Never again."

Chapter Nine

Nakeisha paced within the confines of her quarters. She was dressed in one of her silver silk ceremonial robes, her black hair confined neatly in a braid that hung down her back. She was clean, she was fed, and she was safe, at least for now. So why did she pace like a caged beast?

With a sigh she stopped in front of the viewport and stared out at the stars. She hated deception and withholding information felt very much like deceiving the captain and his crew. She could only hope the captain understood why she had withheld certain things from him.

You worry not about the captain's feelings but about the feelings of the tribesman, E.Z. told her.

Nakeisha chose not to respond.

A gentle laugh filled her mind. *There is no shame in having feelings for another.*

"We barely know each other," she snapped. "And I bring nothing but trouble to him and his friends."

It was not your fault he was injured.

"How can you say that? He —"

Enough. Your guilt is misplaced. He had his own mission at the library.

"But I should have trusted—"

Trusted whom? The captain? The crew? And what if you had been wrong? Even I did not know the truth until you were at the library, and by then it was too late, events had already been set into motion.

Nakeisha sighed. E.Z. was correct, as usual.

"So how much do I tell them now?"

I leave it to your discretion, my dear friend.

"Thanks," she muttered. Taking a deep breath she started towards the door.

Wait.

"What is it?"

In the bags sent from the library you will find a black case.

Curious, she went over to the bags stacked in the corner of the room and searched until she found the black case.

Open it.

Still mystified, she did as she was told. Nestled in the soft, black lining was a set of five balls made of metal and glass. One of them would fill the palm of her hand. They glowed with an inner light, seeming almost to pulse.

"They're beautiful. Are they a gift for the captain?"

They are eoflessi. Keep one for your own use and gift the cap-tain with the others to do with as he will.

"Privacy orbs," she mused, turning one over in her hands. "I've heard of them, of course, but I've never seen one, until now. I'm sure the captain will make good use of your gift."

That's the idea, E.Z. said.

"Will you sit down? You're making me tired just watching you," Captain Blake said, watching Chaney pacing back and forth across his cabin.

"Sorry, Cap," Chaney flopped down in the chair across from him. He had a fresh dressing on his wound, fresh clothing, and had even time for a shower. Other than being a little tired, he felt fine.

"Why don't we start with your version of what really happened?" the captain suggested. "I'm sure there was more to it than the story you gave in the corridor."

"A little more," Chaney admitted. "We got there and were taken to a room to wait in. Then one of the library technicians came in and was totally shocked when he saw Nakeisha."

"So she did have friends at the library?"

Chaney hesitated. "I don't know if I'd call them friends. The way he acted . . . he recognized her, that was for certain, but it was like she was someone of importance and her appearance was totally unexpected."

"Hmm," the captain stroked his beard. "What happened next?"

"Then he whisked Nakeisha away and I was left there to wait until one of the Librarians came to me. He told me something called the *ardraci* was being prepared for transport but then the library came under attack before he could give it to me."

"How'd you meet up with Nakeisha again?"

"That's the strange part. The Librarian took me deeper into the library so I could hide in a secret room until it was safe to leave. The next thing I know, Nakeisha's being hidden in the same room. After the bombing died down one of the technicians came to let us out and led us straight into a trap. We managed to escape and almost made it to the ship before we were caught again."

"I wonder why they hid you in the same place," the captain mused.

There was a soft knock on the captain's door.

"I guess we're about to find out," Chaney said.

Blake went to the door and opened it to let Nakeisha in. Chaney's eyes widened in appreciation. The shimmering grey robe she wore matched her eyes and lent her a regal appearance. It enveloped her completely but did nothing to hide her slender curves.

"How are you feeling?" the captain asked.

"Much better, thank you," she said, slanting a quick glance Chaney's way.

"I think it's time for us to be honest with each other," he continued. "I'd like–"

She held up one slim hand to stop him. "I would like to present you with a gift, Captain."

"That's not necessary–"

"Oh, but I think you will agree that it is." She set the black case on the table and opened it. Picking up one of the delicate looking spheres, she turned one of the metal bands counter-clockwise and then set the sphere on the table.

"These are called *eoflessi*, also known as privacy orbs by my people," she told the two men.

"I've heard of these," Blake said, carefully picking one up to examine it. "They're a very rare piece of Ilezie organic technology."

"Organic?" Chaney asked in surprise.

"They are simple to operate," Nakeisha continued. "Turn the band a half turn clockwise to muffle sound, a full turn to block sound completely. To mask a conversation, turn the band counter clockwise."

"What do you mean, mask a conversation," Chaney asked, picking one up and turning it around carefully in his hands. It was much heavier than he expected.

"The *eoflessi* has the ability to take a private conversation and turn it into something mundane." She shook her head as Chaney opened his mouth again, "Don't ask me how it is able to do this, I am no scientist, but it will work against even the hardest to detect listening devices."

"Even one is worth a small fortune," the captain mused, still turning the sphere around in his hands. "Four of them . . . I could buy a whole planet with four of them."

"If that is your wish, Captain," Nakeisha said, taking a seat.

He glanced at her sharply. "I take it this means you're ready to share your story with Chaney and me?"

"I find it difficult to know where to start," she said honestly. "So much has happened in such a short time . . ."

Now that's an understatement if ever I heard one, E.Z. said.

You're not helping! She thought back at him. The whole situation was making her extremely uncomfortable. Would they be annoyed that she withheld information from them? Angry that she put them all in danger?

"Those men at the library," Chaney said slowly. "They weren't after me; they were after you, weren't they?"

"I believe so, yes." She sighed and drew her feet up to curl underneath her. "The world I come from is very distant. The name would mean nothing to you. We have been under the protection of the Ilezie for generations, but the Ilezie have decided that the time has come for us to take our place in the Pan-Galactic Council of Worlds. I was chosen by them to represent my world."

"Your people are one of the lost races?" Blake asked.

Nakeisha hesitated.

Tell them, E.Z. ordered.

"Yes. I am Ardraci, an Elemental."

Both men stared at her.

"My companion and I were journeying to the Council when we were attacked. Though it was the T'tenet who captured and tortured us, I believe it was under the direction of someone else."

"You're the package the Council sent us to Tersic to pick up!" Chaney said suddenly. It all made so much sense now, the library technician's reaction to her, the reason they were hidden in the same room together—he should have figured it out for himself.

"That's correct," she smiled ruefully. "I knew only that I needed to get to the library and that arrangements had been made. If I had known my transportation was to be the Comet I could have saved us both a great deal of trouble."

Tell them the rest, E.Z. demanded.

Nakeisha sighed. "There is something else you must know. I am also *Illarie* - a vessel. I carry within me the essence, or soul, if you will, of my Ilezie companion."

"I'm not sure I understand what that means," Blake admitted.

"What it means, gentlemen, is that if I am captured, I must have your word you will kill me.

Chapter Ten

The silence in the captain's cabin was absolute as both men stared at Nakeisha.

Chaney was the first one to break it. "That's the stupidest thing I've ever heard!"

A little dramatic, don't you think? E.Z. whispered at the same time.

Nakeisha ignored them both.

"The knowledge my Ilezie companion had is invaluable. It cannot be allowed to fall into enemy hands."

Do not underestimate your own worth.

"As a representative of one of the Old Races, you, yourself, would make a valuable hostage," the captain said, "But I cannot in good conscience–"

"Your death would solve nothing," Chaney broke in. "Where there is life, there is hope."

The tribesman has a point, E.Z. agreed.

Nakeisha sighed. "While I agree in principle, the truth is I am a conduit through which many secrets of the Ilezie may be accessed. You both know there are methods of extracting information from an unwilling mind."

Highly illegal and immoral methods, E.Z. put in.

"And I think you will agree that even though these methods are illegal, this does not stop them from being used."

Chaney opened his mouth to disagree, then closed it again. What she said was true, and both he and the captain knew it. But it didn't mean he had to like it, or condone what she was asking.

"Well," Blake said, after several moments of consideration. "I think we'll just have to agree not to let you fall into enemy hands."

Nakeisha opened her mouth to argue.

Let it go, E.Z. told her.

Her mouth snapped shut again. But–

If the time comes when all hope is lost, I will make sure any knowledge you carry remains inviolate.

You can do that?

You would be surprised at what I can do.

Chaney watched her carefully. She seemed to be having some kind of internal struggle. He wondered what it would be like to convey the soul of another. It seemed like a heavy burden to carry.

"This being a vessel," he said. "Is this a common thing amongst your people?"

"No," she shook her head. "In fact it is quite rare. Only one in a thousand has the ability to become *Illarie*, and not all who have the ability are ever needed to use it." In fact, she had never known anyone who was *Illarie*, filled or not.

How did the under-librarian know I was Illarie when I did not? She asked E.Z.

To be a Librarian on Tersic is to also be a priest. They are much more than they appear to be and have abilities even the Ilezie do not fully understand.

The captain stroked his beard thoughtfully. "You may have realized we've been having some difficulties on our mission for the council," he began.

Chaney snorted.

"I feel I must warn you that I've come to believe we have a spy on the ship. There have been too many close calls, too many coincidences . . ."

I suspected as much, E.Z. said.

"Have you a suspect?" she asked.

"No. I know I can trust Chaney and I can only presume I can trust you as well."

"You trust Chaney because he is from Soporo, and a Fedylian?" she shot a quick glance at the man in question. "I mean no offense, I am just curious."

"Chaney and I have worked together for years. I've never met a more honorable man, Fedylian or not."

She nodded thoughtfully.

"So what's our next move?" Chaney asked. Far from being offended by Nakeisha's question, he admired her forthrightness.

"The last communication I had with our contact ordered us to bring the package we picked up on Tersic to the Council."

I would not advise a direct route, E.Z. said.

"I would suggest we do not take a direct route," Nakeisha said. "It might be suspect."

"No one else on board knew we were supposed to pick up a package, right Cap?" Chaney asked thoughtfully.

"That's right."

"Then I suggest we pretend to stick to our original mission, to seek out one of the Old Races, and take a route that spirals into Council friendly space. Right now we're about as far from the Council as we can get and still be in known space."

An excellent plan, E.Z. concurred.

"How do you explain my presence on board?" Nakeisha asked.

"That's easy," Captain Blake said. "I was feeling guilty because you got caught up in our troubles and offered you free passage back to Council territory."

"An excellent plan," she agreed.

"Now all we have to do is avoid the spy, Corporate, Sector, and pirates on our way to the Council," Chaney said. "Should be no problem at all."

Chaney insisted on walking Nakeisha back to her quarters, but he had become reserved, treating her with an unwarranted formality. Was it because she was Ardraci, from one of the lost worlds? There were many who considered the Old Races, steeped in history and tradition, to be inferior. She had not thought Chaney to be one of them. There was a sharp sting of regret at the loss of easy comradeship between them.

When they reached her door she turned to him. "I am sorry that you became injured on my behalf," she said a little awkwardly, unable to meet his eye. "I can only apologize that you and your friends have become embroiled in my troubles."

With that she slipped inside her room, leaving him staring at her in surprise.

"Wait a minute," he said. He caught the door before it could shut and followed her inside. "Do you think I blame you for my getting shot?"

It was her turn to look surprised. It was exactly what she thought. What else was she to think when he was suddenly so stiff and formal with her. "But I–"

"It's a foolish thought," he told her. "You were not the one wielding the laser that shot me."

"But–"

He reached her in two steps and laid a hand across her lips. "The trouble we are in is not of your making. Trust me in this."

He is right, E.Z. agreed. *None of this is of your making.*

Nakeisha hesitated and then nodded. Chaney took his hand away.

She sighed and turned away. "It is hard not to feel responsible. So much ill has been done - death, torture, the destruction of the Great Library . . ."

He came up behind her as she stared out the view port and rested his hands on her shoulders. "We don't know for certain that you're what they were after in the library, and didn't you say it was the Ilezie's decision, not yours, to meet with the council?"

If anyone is responsible, it is I, E.Z. said suddenly. *I am the one who chose you for this task.*

All right, she thought back at him. *I cannot argue with both of you!*

"You are right, of course," she said with another sigh.

He gave her shoulders a squeeze and let go.

"Why don't we sit down?" she suggested.

"You knew about the spy before Cap said anything, didn't you?" he asked when they were comfortable. "That's why you gave him the *eoflessi*."

She shot him a surprised glance, then looked quickly away. "Not as such, no. But it seemed a wise precaution to take, given the importance of the mission."

"The mission," he echoed. "I wonder if the Council knew of your presence all along?"

Nakeisha shook her head. "It is unlikely. We traveled in secret, as much as we were able."

"Pretty hard to keep an Ilezie secret. They're exceptionally distinctive in appearance."

"This is true," she agreed.

It was a calculated risk, E.Z. told her.

You might have warned me!

"You said you're both Ardraci and an Elemental. Aren't they the same thing?"

"Yes, and no. All Ardraci have the potential to become Elementals, but not all wish to undergo the training. It takes many years."

"What exactly is an Elemental? Is it like royalty?" He wanted to take the words back the moment he said them but tried not to let his embarrassment show.

She laughed, music to his ears. "Do not let the fine clothes fool you. Elementals are not so illustrious, or uncommon. There are many of us; we vary in both strength and skill. I do not know why I was chosen for this task."

E.Z. appeared to have nothing to say on the matter.

"What kind of skills? No, wait. You're an Elemental, and your name is Windsinger. Your power lies in the air, right? Or more specifically, the wind."

"That is correct," she said, pleased he was able to figure it out.

His eyes widened suddenly. "The wind storm down on Tersic, that was your doing?"

Nakeisha blushed slightly. "My control is imperfect, especially when I am feeling strong emotions."

He opened his mouth and then shut it again quickly.

"What is it?"

"Nothing," he mumbled.

She looked at him steadily, but he refused to meet her eyes. "Ah. I think I know what it is. You are wondering if I was responsible for the weather on Temus, where we first met."

"I'm sor—"

"The answer is yes. I was . . . not myself, and I created the storm out of my anger. It was not one of my most shining moments," she admitted.

"I think I can understand how you were feeling," he said slowly. "I can't say that I would have done any different in your place."

"Thank you, Chaney. Your understanding means a great deal to me."

They sat in silence for a time, each wrapped in their own thoughts.

"What are you thinking?" Nakeisha asked softly.

Chaney started, flushing slightly. "I'm sorry. My mind was elsewhere for a moment."

She waited patiently.

"I was thinking of the way you fought in the Library, it was quite impressive. I've never seen that style of combat before. Is it common where you're from?"

"Though we are a passive people by nature, we are taught defensive skills from an early age."

"I was hop–"

A crackle from the ships intercom system startled them both. "Chaney, report to the bridge."

"I'm sorry," he said with genuine regret as he rose. "We'll have to finish this later."

"I, more than most, understand what it means when duty calls," she assured him, rising as well.

He hesitated at the door, "Perhaps, if you're feeling up to it, we could have a sparring match in a day or two. You could show me some of those moves."

A smile lit up her face, "I would enjoy that."

"It's a date then," he said with a smile, door sliding shut behind him.

Chapter Eleven

Chaney stood framed in the doorway of the exercise room, watching as Nakeisha ran through a series of complicated stretching exercises. She was dressed in form fitting black, the pliant material hugging every curve. Her hair was confined in a neat braid that coiled around her head.

"You should be stretching as well," she said without looking at him.

Chagrined, he finished entering the room so the door slid shut behind him.

"These movements are called the *psharbon,* the prelude."

"Prelude to what?" he asked, joining her on the mats.

Without halting, she said, "To battle, of course."

The movements were so simple and fluid that he was lulled into believing they were easy. After a few minutes of it, however, he started to feel the pull in his muscles. When they were finished warming up they stood facing each other on the mat.

Nakeisha bounced gently on her feet. "How shall we proceed?" she asked.

"I've never sparred with a woman before," Chaney admitted.

"Don't think of me as a woman, think of me as the enemy."

He raised a brow but wisely kept his mouth shut. Dressed as she was, there was no way he would be able to forget she was a woman.

As first they merely circled each other, neither wanting to go on the offensive. Nakeisha's patience ran out first. She feinted a blow to his head that spun into a kick that glanced off his shoulder. He grunted from the impact but before he could do more she put her shoulder to his torso and flipped him neatly over her back. He landed on his back with a thud.

"Are we going to fight or dance?" she asked.

His lips tightened but he made no reply as he flipped up onto his feet again. Eyes narrowed, he stayed focused. This time he was the aggressor. He tried every trick he knew, but he was unable to break through her defenses. A change of strategy was called for.

Pretending to stumble, he allowed her to clip him twice on the side of the head. He shook his head as though to clear it and she closed in, taking the bait. In seconds he had her in a wrestler's hold.

"Do you yield?" he asked, panting in her ear.

"Never!"

To his surprise, she was able to slither out of his grasp. He made another grab for her and missed. She responded with a series of lightning fast jabs that had him backing peddling to stay out of her reach. Her foot swept up and connected with his side.

With a gasp of pain, Chaney went down. Nakeisha stared at him in surprise, then her eyes widened as he made no move to rise again.

"Oh, Chaney, forgive me! I forgot about your injury."

Falling to her knees beside him, she reached out to the hand that was pressed to his side. His other hand snaked out and caught her by the wrist. Before she realized what was happening, he had her flipped onto her back, pinned beneath him.

He grinned down at the surprise on her face. "Now do you yield?"

"You cheated," she said, breathlessly.

"I improvised."

Her breath hitched as she suddenly became aware of his weight on her. It was not unwelcome, just . . . unexpected. His eyes darkened as she wriggled experimentally beneath him. His head moved closer to hers. When his lips were a hair's breadth away from hers she whispered, "I yield."

Chaney's grin faded as he looked into Nakeisha's eyes and saw his own desire reflected back at him.

"I accept your surrender," he whispered back.

He kissed her slowly, allowing her the chance to pull away. She didn't, instead she began to kiss him back. He groaned, deep in his throat, and tightened his grip. Her arms crept up around his neck and he had the sensation of being caught up in a whirlwind.

"Chaney, are you in here?"

Nakeisha's eyes snapped open and she froze in shock. Chaney's quick reflexes kicked in and in one smooth movement he rolled off her and rose, offering his hand to help her up.

"Over here," he called, grateful for the room's L-shape that had hidden them from view.

They were both flushed and a little winded, but by the time Libby rounded the corner they were on their feet and several inches apart. "Are you two all right?"

"Why wouldn't we be?" Chaney asked with a frown.

They were both mature adults and what they chose to do together was no one else's concern. It wasn't as if he'd taken advantage of Nakeisha. Well, maybe he had taken advantage of the situation just a little, but she certainly hadn't protested. And in any case, it was between her and him.

"You didn't notice the fans were malfunctioning?" Libby asked, oblivious to the undercurrents. "You were lucky you weren't hit with anything. What were you doing, anyway?"

Chaney looked around them and only then realized that the whirlwind sensation he'd felt had been real. The room looked like a disaster zone. Nakeisha paled as she took in the damage.

"There was no malfunction," Chaney said carefully. "It was my fault, I wanted to try and recreate the conditions on Tersic to see if we could have found a better fighting strategy."

"And what are the odds that you'd be fighting under the same conditions some day?" Libby asked. She held up a hand and shook her head ruefully when he would have answered. "Never mind, just so long as you clean up when you're finished."

"You were looking for me?" he asked pointedly. He and Nakeisha needed to talk about what had happened.

"Right," Libby swung her attention back to him. "Cap has finally decided on our next port of call and he needs you to plot the course."

"I'll get right on it," he promised. "Just as soon as we clean up in here."

Nakeisha laid a hand on his arm. There was a part of her that wanted very much to finish what they'd started, but another part of her was appalled at the fact she'd caused so much wind damage without being aware of it. Until she was able to figure out what happened she would avoid being alone with Chaney.

"Please, attend your duties. I can see to this." It was the least she could do since she was the cause of it.

"But—" He wasn't ready to leave her yet.

"I will be fine," she said with a reassuring smile. "I am the only one without duties on this ship. I find that time lies heavy on my hands with nothing to do. This will be a nice change."

"If you're sure . . ."

"I am sure," she said decisively.

"Don't let Cap know you're looking for something to do," Libby warned with a laugh, "He's liable to put you to work."

Nakeisha shrugged. "If there is anything I could do to help, I would be most happy to do it."

"I'll let Cap know," Libby promised.

At the same time, Chaney frowned. "Are you sure that's a good idea?" Nakeisha was a diplomat, even if no one else knew it. And from the way the Librarians treated her she was an important person in her own right, despite her protests to the contrary. She shouldn't be made to pitch in and help around the ship.

Both women looked at him in surprise. He fidgeted under their scrutiny.

"I just figured since you're Cap's guest you might have other things you'd rather do. It's not like we're not making out okay on our own," he finished lamely.

"I thank you for your concern," Nakeisha said, a little formally. For a few brief seconds in his arms she thought he'd seen beyond what she was, but perhaps she'd been mistaken. "But I am sure that Captain Blake would not ask of me anything too taxing. I cannot spend the whole of the journey in my cabin meditating."

"Of course not," Libby assured her.

But it was not Libby she was looking to for reassurance.

Chapter Twelve

As the door slid closed behind Libby and Chaney, Nakeisha turned and surveyed the disarray of the room.

You have no reason to be angry.

It was more of a statement than a question, but she chose to address it.

"I'm not angry so much as discouraged," she admitted with a sigh. "I thought my control was much better than this."

Your control of your element, or of your emotions?

Ignoring the question, she began setting the room to rights.

After a few moments, E.Z. continued. *This problem is not something that can just be ignored. It must be addressed.*

"What problem is that?" she asked irritably, continuing to straighten equipment. She shoved an exercise mat back into place with her foot.

The problem of having your emotional well being tied to the control of your element.

Nakeisha flushed slightly. She finished cleaning up and then sat down on the floor, back against the wall.

"Are you suggesting that I stay away from Chaney?" she asked finally.

Quite the contrary, E.Z. told her. *Of everyone on this ship, he is probably the safest for you to spend time with. He already knows you're Ardraci, he can be trusted to keep your secret.*

"What am I going to do, E.Z.? How can I go in front of the council if I have so little control that I create a wind storm just because a man kisses me?"

You must learn better control of your power.

"You make it sound so easy . . ."

It will not be easy. It will take much practice, and even more patience.

"What if I can't do it?" she asked in a small voice.

Then your power will rip you apart, he said bluntly.

She had barely enough time to digest this piece of information when the door to the workout room slid open.

"So this is where you're hiding," Nigel exclaimed.

"Not hiding," Nakeisha said, mustering up a smile for him. "Just resting from a workout. Chaney and I had a sparring match earlier."

Nigel frowned. "No wonder you look so pale, sparring with Chaney would take it out of anyone."

He offered her a hand to help her up, keeping a hold of it once she was on her feet. Tucking her hand under his arm he began to lead her to the door.

"Where are we going?"

"As your doctor, I prescribe a drink in the dining hall."

"A drink?"

"With yours truly, of course," he said with a smile.

"Of course," she murmured, allowing him to lead her from the room. The moving parts of the exercise machines swayed slightly, as though in a light breeze.

"So," Nigel said, once they were sitting down with drinks in front of them. "Libby tells me that you're thinking of asking the captain to assign you some duties."

"The captain has been so kind offering me transport, I feel I must repay him in some fashion," she said carefully.

She'd have to watch herself with Nigel. While his attention to her was flattering, she found his attitude somewhat overbearing. It would be all too easy to lose her temper with him. And she well knew what happened the last time she lost her temper.

There were extenuating circumstances, E.Z. said gently.

I can't take the chance, she responded.

She could feel E.Z. was unhappy with her answer, but he stayed silent. All at once she realized Nigel had stopped talking and was staring at her expectantly.

"I'm sorry, my mind was elsewhere for a moment," she said. "What were you saying?"

"I was asking how much you liked plants. If it's all right with the captain you could take over looking after the hydroponics bay."

"I think I would enjoy that," Nakeisha said with a genuine smile.

"Great," he smiled back. "When would you like to start?"

"As they say, there is no time like the present," she finished her drink and rose. "What must I do?"

"First stop is the bridge to get the captain's official authorization, then I'll take you down to the bay and show you what to do."

"Thank you, Nigel. You are most kind."

"No, thank you. You have no idea how much I hate gardening!"

"Vida, have a look at this."

Chaney had finished plotting their course and frowned as he focused on the long range monitor in front of him.

"What have you got?" Vida asked. She moved to peer over his shoulder.

"Wait for it . . . There!" he pointed. "Did you see that?"

"I saw something," she agreed. "What do you think it is?"

"I don't know, but it's been appearing just on the edge of our scan for the last hour."

Vida flipped the intercom switch. "Captain to the bridge."

They stood shoulder to shoulder watching the monitor while they waited for the captain. It didn't take him long to join them.

"What are we looking at?" he asked.

"We're not sure, Cap," Vida answered, without taking her eyes off the screen. "I'd like to say it's just a sensor shadow, but I doubt it's anything that innocent."

"It doesn't seem to be trying to move any closer," Chaney said. "In fact, it looks to me like whatever it is just wants to follow, not intercept."

"We've tried minor course and speed adjustments," Vida put in, "But it stays just out of scanning range."

"I don't like it," the Captain said after watching for a few minutes. "Vida, do we still have any of those sneaker probes we picked up on Perig?"

"Two of them, sir."

"Good. Deploy one in full stealth mode. Let's see if we can get a look at what's following us. Chaney, I want you search for possible escape routes, just in case we have to make a run for it."

"Aye, Captain."

The two got to work. Vida programmed the probe and sent it on its way while Chaney did a full sweep of the sector. There weren't many options - an asteroid field, a class two nebula, the nearest inhabited planet was light years away. One of the reasons he'd chosen this route is because there was less chance of running into anyone.

Before he was finished his scans, there was already information coming in from the probe.

"Receiving probe data, Cap," Vida told him.

"Well?" he asked impatiently when she paused.

"Sorry, sir, it's just . . . I'm not familiar with this ship configuration."

"But it's definitely a ship?"

"Yes sir, probe data confirms it. Checking specifications now."

Her fingers flew over the panel in front of her. "No I.D. strata so it's not a Sector or a Corporate ship."

"Could it be a Council ship sent to help?"

She shook her head. "Negative sir. It fits no known Council configuration. In fact, it doesn't fit any of the configurations in our database."

"Can you get a view of it up on the screen?"

"Yes sir."

Vida sent the order to the probe and the main viewer was filled with an image of the unknown ship. It didn't look much different from the Burning Comet, save that its hull was a dull silver and it was obviously much newer. There were red markings along the hull between the nose and the wing of the craft.

"I don't know if it could outrun us sir, not after those upgrades we got six months ago, but it can definitely outgun us."

"Let's hope it won't come to that," the captain murmured. "Chaney, find anything useful out there?"

"I think our best bet would be the asteroid field," Chaney replied. "We can alter our course without making it seem too obvious and once we're through we can head straight for Straisus."

Captain Blake nodded thoughtfully. "All right, sounds like a plan. Let's do it."

Chaney nodded and plotted the new course.

"Vida, can you get a close up of those markings?"

"I'll see what I can do, Cap."

The view screen wavered for a moment and then zoomed in on the red markings. There was an image of a red bird-like creature with spread wings, followed by some lettering.

"Libby?" the captain asked.

Libby eyed the screen for a moment and then shook her head. "Sorry, Captain. It looks vaguely familiar, but I really couldn't say for sure."

The door to the bridge swooshed open and Nakeisha entered, accompanied by Nigel.

Nakeisha paled and took several steps towards the view screen. "*Ves'ti'stus!*"

The three men turned to Libby for an interpretation.

"Literally, it means something unpleasant is about

to hit the air outtake system."

Chapter Thirteen

"I think they realize we've seen them," Chaney reported. "They're headed our way and making no effort to hide."

"You recognize that ship?" the captain asked.

Nakeisha was staring at the screen as though mesmerized. She shivered, and turned to the captain. This was the very last thing they needed.

"It belongs to the Deraidne, they are an order of religious zealots."

"I've never heard of them before," Chaney said.

The captain opened his mouth to ask what religious zealots could possibly want with them, but realized the answer was probably standing right in front of him.

"Try to contact them," Blake told Libby. "Let them know we're just a peaceful trading vessel and we don't want any trouble."

Libby focused on the communications console. After a few, tense, moments she turned back again. "They're receiving our message, but there's no response."

"All right, people," Blake said. "I'd like to avoid trouble if I can, but just in case . . . Vida, I need you down in the engine room. Libby – go with her. Nigel, get down to the med-lab and make sure everything's secure."

"Aye, Captain," they responded, almost simultaneously. When the Captain gave orders in that tone of voice he expected to be obeyed without question.

"Chaney, I'll need you here with me. And you," he directed at Nakeisha, "I want you to tell me everything you know about these Deraidne.

"They exist primarily to spread the word of Deraid so that everyone lives their lives according to the twelve laws. That symbol," she nodded at the red bird still displayed on the view screen, "is the avatar of Deraid. They believe that at the appointed time the avatar will rise and strike down all non-believers."

"How much of a threat do they pose?"

She hesitated. "If they believe this ship poses a threat, they will not hesitate to attack. If they know I am aboard they will make sure this ship and everyone on it is destroyed."

"What could they possibly have against you?" Chaney asked

"My people have been at war with the Deraidne for many years. They both hate and fear the Ardraci, because of our power over the elements. They are fierce fighters," she continued. "They do not believe in taking prisoners, and they will give their lives freely in the name of their cause."

"I've come up against religious zealots before," the captain said slowly. "There's nothing worse. Not only don't they fear death, they almost welcome it."

"They're starting to close the gap," Chaney reported.

Captain Blake swore under his breath. "How close are we to the asteroid field?"

"We might just make it."

Chaney's fingers danced over the controls, trying to squeeze every last ounce of speed out of the ship. A red light lit up on the sensor panel and a warning tone sounded.

"Brace for impact!"

The ship shook as it was hit by a blast from the Deraidne.

A solar wind is so powerful, it has large effects on the tails of comets. It even has measurable effects on the trajectories of spacecraft.

What? Nakeisha thought back.

Focus.

Are you mad? You know what happened on Temus, I couldn't possibly control a solar wind!

Which is worse, to die trying or to die doing nothing?

Nakeisha stared at the view screen again. The image of the Deraidne ship had been replaced by a forward view of space. The asteroid field seemed a million light years away. They weren't going to make it. She griped the edge of the console to steady herself.

Taking a deep breath, she closed her eyes and reached out with her mind. She could almost feel the coldness of space surrounding her. It was so vast, a never-ending expanse. It would be so easy to lose oneself in it. The ship rocked as another blast hit it and her eyes snapped open.

Again! Concentrate!

I can't!

Then die.

Her mind recoiled from the coldness in E.Z.'s voice. Despair washed over her, followed by anger. He was supposed to be her friend, her teacher, and now he was stuck in her head like some parasite, intruding in her thoughts. How dare he judge her!

With steely determination she focused on the view in front of her and stilled her thoughts, pushing everything else aside. Expanding her awareness, she embraced the cold emptiness of space, seeking the solar winds. They were elusive, faint tendrils, wisps of nothingness. They were far from any sun, too weak to be an effective deterrent.

Reaching deep within herself, she fed them power, building up a small, whirling mass of energy. The Deraidne ship appeared as a cold blue mass in her mind's eye and she sent the whirl wind of energy hurtling towards it. The ship had just fired again, but the blast was caught up in the swirling vortex of energy and propelled back towards it.

The flash was blinding, even with the protection of the blast shields.

Nakeisha's mind went dark.

Chaney turned away from the console to see Nakeisha slither to the floor in a boneless heap. It was a credit to his speed that he reached her side in time to prevent her head from hitting the deck.

"What just happened?" Captain Blake asked.

"I don't know, Cap. One second we were about to get hit again, and the next thing I know the Deraidne ship is exploding."

"Now what? Is she all right?"

"I think she just fainted," Chaney said, checking her pulse. She looked pale, but then she seemed to be naturally pale.

"This is too much of a coincidence," the captain muttered. "You don't think—"

"I don't know what to think, Cap."

"Maybe we should let Nigel know what's going on, he could check her out."

Chaney opened his mouth to agree, but instead found himself saying, "I don't think the doctor is necessary, I'm pretty sure all she needs is rest."

"All right," Blake agreed, attention focused on the debris field in front of them. "Take her to her quar-

ters, I can manage here. And maybe you should stay
with her until she wakes up, just to be on the safe
side."

"Aye, sir."

Chaney scooped up the unconscious woman and
left the bridge quickly. She was a featherweight in his
arms. The distance to the guest quarters was short
and he was grateful he didn't run into anyone. He
couldn't explain the sudden urge to keep her away
from everyone else, even the doctor.

Once safely inside her quarters he took a quick
glance around, wondering where to put her. He shied
away from the bedroom and settled for laying her
carefully on the sofa. After making sure she was comfortable he pulled up a chair and sat down to wait.

Nigel slammed the cabinet door shut and made
sure it was secure. It didn't matter that ship's protocol
stated that in the event of an attack all medical per-
sonnel were to report to the medical facilities, something else was going on. He was being deliberately
kept in the dark, he could smell it. The room vibrated
from the impact of the ship being fired on.

It could have been worse, he could have been sent
to the engine room with Libby and Vida. At least the
med-lab was the most secure place on the ship during
a firefight. A quick check to make sure the magnetic
locks securing the equipment were engaged and he

was finished, just in time for the ship to rock from another direct hit.

Sitting down at his desk he pulled a bottle of whiskey from his bottom drawer and poured himself a shot. Cap and Chaney could have their Hyrodian brandy, whiskey was a real man's drink. Tossing back the first shot he poured another to sip slowly.

Something changed since they'd been to Tersic and he'd bet it had something to do with Nakeisha. Without knowing what really happened down there he found it hard to believe she was as innocent as she appeared. But then she wasn't really innocent, she'd already admitted to attacking the T'tenet, which led to the death of Tavis. The others appeared to have forgotten this, but he hadn't.

He went to take another sip of his drink and realized with surprise he'd finished it. Filling up his glass again he held it up to let the light filter through the amber liquid.

"Here's to you, Tavis," he said solemnly.

It wasn't like Cap to take on passengers, especially during a mission. Yes, there were extenuating circumstances, but their mission for the Council was supposed to be a priority. Which brought his contemplation around to their mission. They were supposed to be searching for the lost worlds, but hadn't stayed at Tersic long enough to dig up anything.

Cap had overseen the loading of the supplies waiting for them on Tersic. There must have been something in the supplies that he didn't want anyone else to see, but what? And who had attacked Chaney at the library, or was it really Nakeisha they'd been after?

Questions and more questions, and very few answers. Nigel finished his drink and put the bottle away. He had a feeling he was going to need all his wits about him in the days to come.

Chapter Fourteen

Chaney watched Nakeisha as she slept. She looked young and fragile, and there were faint shadows beneath her eyes again. He thought of everything she'd told him and the captain, and wondered how much of what happened to the alien ship was her doing. It seemed almost unbelievable, but there was no other possible explanation.

Such a terrible power, what must it be like to wield it? She claimed to have little control, but for her to be able to move a ship must have taking an astonishing amount of control. He was still lost in thought when she finally stirred.

"How are you feeling?" he asked.

"Tired," she admitted, sitting up slowly. "Tired and ashamed. I meant only to gain us time to escape, I did not intend the destruction of the Deraidne ship."

"You were able to manipulate the solar winds, weren't you?"

"I should not have done so. I have never heard of anyone doing so before and now I know why."

You were not at fault, E.Z. said.

"You can't blame yourself," Chaney said at the same time.

"All those lives lost," she said, eyes haunted.

You had no way of knowing the ship was about to fire.

"The ship must have fired at the same time your winds pushed at it. You're not the one who destroyed them, they destroyed themselves."

She refused to be mollified. Getting up, she went over to the view port and stood looking out at the asteroid field. Chaney rose as well and went over to stand behind her, resting his hands on her shoulders. E.Z.'s presence vanished from her mind.

"If that last shot had reached us, it would have destroyed the ship," Chaney said.

"Perhaps . . ."

He turned her gently around so she was facing him.

"You saved our lives," he told her, then kissed her softly.

She shivered, and then pressed closer to his warmth. His hands slipped from her shoulders to her back and he pulled her tight against him, deepening the kiss. Her mouth opened under his and his whole body tightened in response.

Together they sank back down onto the sofa. Her arms went around him, hands stroking his shoulders and back. Chaney broke off the kiss and with a groan buried his face in her hair.

"We have to stop," he said, heart thundering in his ears.

"Why?" she asked breathlessly. She kissed his neck and jaw, hands threading through his hair to draw him closer again.

"I'm still on duty." He kissed the hollow of her throat then gently took the lobe of her ear between his teeth.

Nakeisha gasped pressing closer into his touch. "When is your duty finished?"

"Not soon enough."

He framed her face with his hands and went back to kissing her. Before he could lose himself again, he pulled away once more.

"I really should be going," he said, voice heavy with regret.

"Yes, your duty," she murmured, reluctantly releasing him. She bit her lip and looked at him uncertainly.

He took her hands in his and kissed the back of them. "What is it?"

She couldn't look him in the eye as she said, "When you're duty is finished, that is, when you are free . . . your presence would be most welcome should you decide to return later."

Her sudden shyness touched him deeper than anything else. Placing a finger under her chin he raised
her head so that she was looking right at him. He
couldn't resist kissing her one more time before saying, "It would please me to find a welcome here
should I return after my duty is completed."

Nakeisha couldn't help smiling at the formal tone
he adopted.

"I will be waiting," she said.

Nakeisha was still smiling as the door closed after
Chaney. This entire journey had been one disaster
after another. It was nice to have something to look
forward to for a change.

She wandered over to the view port but found the
display of the asteroid field uninteresting. Restless,
she went back over to the sofa and settled down to
meditate. After a few minutes she opened her eyes
with a sigh. With them closed all she could think
about was the way Chaney's arms had felt around her.

Time seemed to crawl without him. She needed
something to do to make it go faster.

Her stomach chose that moment to give a slight
rumble, reminding her of how long it had been since
she'd last eaten. With no day or night in space it was
all too easy to lose track of time. She could have a
quick bite to eat and bring back a snack for later. Perhaps Chaney would hungry after his duty was over.

Pleased with her plan, she left immediately. There
was no one in the dining hall when she entered, but as

she studied the instructions on the food processing unit she was joined by Libby.

"Having problems?" Libby asked with a smile.

"The difficulty with an F.P.U. is that it can make any meal I wish. I find I cannot decide what to choose."

Libby's smile broadened. "When I first joined the crew of the Comet, I gained ten pounds for that very reason. I couldn't decide what to choose, so I chose everything."

Laughing, Nakeisha said, "I do not think I could manage everything, I am more in the mood for something light."

"If I may make a suggestion?"

"Please do."

Libby typed instructions into the control panel and pressed the generate button. The dispensing slot opened and she reached in to remove two heaping plates.

"That smells good," Nakeisha said appreciatively as she followed Libby to a table. "What is it?"

"It's called *miksaub*, it's considered quite a delicacy on my world. Of course the processed version can't compare with the real thing, but it's not bad."

"It's delicious," Nakeisha assured her, taking a bite. It was salad-like in appearance, but had the tang of fruit with a slight crunch to it."

"Is that *miksaub* I'm smelling?" Nigel asked, entering the dining hall. "I think that would just hit the spot. Would you ladies mind if I joined you?"

"Not at all," Libby told him.

Nakeisha smiled faintly. While she'd been enjoying Libby's company, she was not in the mood for the doctor's banter.

Nigel programmed his own plate of food and brought it over to their table, seating himself beside Nakeisha.

"Would anyone else like something to drink?" she asked, rising.

When the others assented, she went to the processor and brought back three tall glasses of sapphire liquid.

"This is *haraf*. In its original form it is made from the pressings of the *harafazi* fruit." The others took a cautious sip. Libby smiled, while Nigel seemed a little more reserved.

"This is wonderful," Libby exclaimed. "And it goes perfectly with the *miksaub*."

"It's very . . . nice," Nigel agreed. "A little mild for my taste, but not bad."

Libby rolled her eyes. "If it doesn't have alcohol in it, it's never any better than "not bad" to the good doctor."

"Don't judge what you haven't tried," he retorted.

"I don't understand," Nakeisha said.

"For all the pleasure-loving of the Bedialians, they don't believe in alcoholic beverages."

"You make it sound offensive," Libby said. "I, on the other hand, do not see the point in consuming a chemical substance that makes you lose your self control."

"Bediali, that is the ninth planet of the Mifalen system, is it not? I have heard it is a most beautiful world, both its land and its people."

Libby positively beamed. "Most people have never heard of it before. I'm impressed. How about you, Nakeisha, where are you from?"

"I am from University City, on Uria. My companion and I were on a pilgrimage of knowledge." It was a little disconcerting how easily the lie came to her lips.

"You've come a long way if you're from Uria," Nigel said in sympathy. "What will you do now?"

Nakeisha sighed. "I do not know. It is almost as far to continue the pilgrimage as it is to return. The Captain has generously offered to allow me passage to a less volatile quadrant."

"I think things are almost more unsettled now than they were during the war," Libby said. "Even a small trading vessel like ours isn't safe."

"That's true," Nigel agreed. "You might not be any safer here than you were on your own." He reached across the table towards her hand. "I'm very glad you decided to join us though."

Nakeisha suppressed a shiver, allowing his hand to touch hers briefly before pulling away. "I thank you for the company," she said, rising. "However, I am growing fatigued."

Bidding the two a good evening, she went back to her quarters. By the time she reached them, she really was feeling fatigued. Fatigued and something else.

Something wasn't right. She could feel it but could do nothing about it. She took two steps into her quarters and swayed on her feet. The door slid automatically shut behind her and she leaned back onto it, sliding slowly to the ground.

Something was terribly wrong, but she was helpless to figure out what.

Chapter Fifteen

From birth, the tribes of Chaney's world were taught to keep their emotions in check. That's not to say they didn't experience emotion, they just suppressed the need to act on them. However, Chaney felt almost lighthearted as he made his way to Nakeisha's room. He didn't know what the night would bring, but he hoped they could finish what they started earlier. In one hand he carried a bottle of wine he'd been saving for a special occasion, in the other a pair goblets, one of the few personal possessions he carried with him from his world.

Pausing outside Nakeisha's door, he tucked the bottle under his arm to free up his hand. He rapped sharply and waited. After a few minutes he rapped again. Frowning slightly, he stood back from the door, hesitating. Had she changed her mind? Or maybe she'd fallen asleep . . .

There was still no answer and after another moment of hesitation he turned to leave. At least he tried to leave. Something held him in place. He was suddenly filled with a nameless fear. Something was wrong, something was terribly wrong, and it had something to do with Nakeisha.

He punched a security code into the lock of her door and dropped the wine and goblets as the door slid open and Nakeisha's limp form spilled out into the corridor.

"Nakeisha!"

He knelt beside her, almost afraid to touch her. Her breathing was shallow. She was pale, even more so than usual, and her skin, when he checked her pulse, was cool and damp. At his touch, her eyes flickered open.

"Chaney?" she whispered.

"Save your strength," he said, gathering her in his arms. "I'll get you to the med-lab."

"Poison," she told him, eyes closing again.

A muscle ticked in his jaw as his teeth ground together. Though the med-lab wasn't far, it seemed to take forever to get there. There was no sign of Nigel as he set Nakeisha carefully on the examining table.

"Nigel to the med-lab!" he barked into the intercom.

He paced between the examining table and the door. When Nigel finally arrived, Chaney grabbed him by his shirt front and dragged him over to Na-keisha.

"She's been poisoned," he said.

Nigel frowned, all business. Quickly, he hooked her up to a monitor, then peeled back the lid of her eye to check her responses.

"What kind of poison was used?" he asked.

"I don't know."

"How long ago did she start feeling the effects?"

"I don't know that either," Chaney said miserably.

Nigel shot him a look then concentrated on the monitor.

"We were supposed to get together after my shift," Chaney said, trying to peer over Nigel's shoulder to see the monitor. "When she didn't answer the door, I got a bad feeling."

"Remind me to never scoff at you and your "feelings" again," Nigel told him. "You got her to me just in time. Another hour and it would have been too late."

"Less talk, more doctoring."

Nigel rolled his eyes. "The diagnostic is already creating a cure. Once it's done it'll administer it and then we wait."

"Wait, wait for what?"

"For her to wake up of course."

"I have no patience for this," Chaney muttered.

"I would have never guessed," Nigel said dryly.

The amber light on the monitor went to blue and there was a faint hissing sound as the machine sent drugs into Nakeisha's system to fight the poison. The blue light turned to green and Nigel pulled the machine away.

"How do you know the machine gave her the right drugs?"

"Because it's a very expensive machine and it wouldn't lie to me," Nigel said, exasperated. "She's probably going to be out for awhile. I can call you when she wakes up."

"I'll wait here," Chaney said, pulling a stool over beside the examining table.

Something flickered in the doctor's eyes, but Chaney was too focused on the woman in front of him to notice.

"Suit yourself," Nigel said.

Captain Blake was frowning as he entered the medlab. "How is she?" he asked.

Nigel checked the monitor sitting beside Nakeisha. "The poison's been purged from her system. She'll be a little tired when she wakes up, but she'll be fine."

"Do we know what happened?"

Chaney stirred where he was keeping vigil beside her. "Someone poisoned her, what more is there to know?"

"There's the question of how this happened, and why," the captain said dryly. "Who was the last person to see her?"

"She was fine when I escorted her to her quarters earlier."

Nigel frowned. "She and Libby were already in the dinning hall when I stopped in for a quick bite. We all had *miksaub*."

"You're feeling all right? What about Libby?"

"I don't know about Libby, but I feel fine. And Nakeisha seemed fine when she left us."

"Do you know what kind of poison it was?" Chaney asked.

"According to the diagnostic, it was a thanium derivative."

"Thanium? Where did it come from?"

"Well, to be honest," the doctor looked a little uncomfortable. "We have a supply on board. In diluted form it's harmless to humans, but deadly to biological parasites. I've been using it in the hydroponics bay."

Blake and Chaney stared at him.

"It's very common," he maintained.

"So how did it get from hydroponics to Nakeisha?"

"That I can't tell you. Even in its pure form it's not considered dangerous to most life forms."

"What do you mean, 'most life forms'?" Chaney asked. "What life forms is it dangerous to?"

"Well . . . it's deadly to any of the reptilian species, some of the amphibious ones as well. There's an old myth that the Old Races had no immunity to it, but since they no longer exist it's a little hard to prove."

"What about Nakeisha," Captain Blake asked.

Nigel glanced at her and shrugged. "She could have a trace of one of the affected races in her genetic make-up or she could just suffer from a natural-born intolerance for certain chemicals. I don't have the equipment here to test her properly."

Chaney and the captain exchanged a glance.

"It's lucky Chaney stopped in to see her," he continued.

"Yes, very lucky," the captain echoed. "You're sure she'll be all right?"

"Positive," Nigel assured him. "She should be waking up soon."

"Chaney, if you wouldn't mind staying with Nakeisha, I'd like the doctor to show me where he keeps his supplies for hydroponics."

"Aye, captain."

"Nigel, let's go."

It was a quick walk to the hydroponics bay, spent in brooding silence. Nothing seemed out of place. Nigel led the Captain over to the cabinet where he kept the thanium. The cabinet was unlocked, but the thanium was there.

"Is this cabinet always unlocked?"

"There's never been a reason to lock it."

"Until now," Blake said grimly.

"Yes, sir," Nigel said, snapping the cabinet shut.

"Stay here and check to make sure nothing's missing. Then I want you to check the processing unit to make sure the thanium didn't some how end up in there."

Nigel stiffened slightly at the order, but all he said was, "Aye, Captain."

Chapter Sixteen

After leaving the hydroponics bay, Captain Blake slowly made his way back to the med-lab. His gut told him this was no accident, but what reason could anyone possibly have for harming Nakeisha?

"Has there been any change?" he asked, joining Chaney at her bedside.

"No, sir."

With a sigh, Blake went over and depressed the intercom button. "Libby to the med-lab."

Chaney's eyes were full of questions left unasked. He'd seen that look on the captain's face before and it didn't bode well.

The door slid open and Libby entered. "You wanted to see me sir?"

Blake moved so he was no longer blocking her view of the examining table. Her eyes widened, her face paled. "What happened?" she asked with a gasp. As far as Blake could tell, her shock was genuine.

"I'm hoping you might be able to tell us," the Captain said. "From what we can gather, she was fine until she visited the dining hall."

"Is she going to be all right?" Libby took a step closer.

"Yes, she'll be fine. Now, about what happened in the dining hall . . ."

"Yes, sir." Libby gulped. "She was already in the dining hall when I got there, trying to decide on something to eat. I—I recommended the *miksaub*. Then Nigel joined us and he had the *miksaub* as well. Is Nigel all right?"

"He's fine," Chaney assured her.

"What did the three of you have to drink?" the captain asked.

"It was something Nakeisha programmed into the F.P.U. I think she called it *haraf*. If I may, sir," she continued, hesitantly, "It's not likely Nakeisha's illness comes from anything she ate or drank in the dining hall. Nigel and I had the same things."

"I'm sure you're right," Blake told her. "I just want to make sure I've got all the bases covered. Did she say where she was headed when she left?"

"Just back to her quarters, sir. Nigel and I stayed another half hour or so and then we left too."

"Thank you, Libby. You're dismissed."

"Yes, sir." She paused at the door. "Tell Nakeisha I wish her a speedy recovery." The door slid shut behind her.

"Well," Blake asked, once she was gone. "What do you think?"

"I don't know what to think, Cap. Both Libby and Nigel had the opportunity to slip Nakeisha the thanium, but what would their motive be?"

"Nigel said it's not dangerous to most life forms . . . could someone have been trying to make her ill, just to keep her out of the way for a while?"

"You think Libby might have done this out of, what, jealousy?"

"She is Bedialian," the Captain pointed out. "And they're used to being the centre of attention. She might have seen Nakeisha as a rival."

Chaney frowned. "I thought Libby took the Oath of Ne'shen, the celibacy vow."

The Captain shrugged. "That doesn't mean she can't feel slighted because the attention has shifted from her."

"I don't know, Cap. Nigel knew it only affected certain life forms, but did Libby? Maybe," he said thoughtfully, "someone was testing to see if she could be from one of the Old Races."

They both stared down at the still figure on the examining table.

"I don't like feeling this way," the Captain said at last. Chaney looked at him inquiringly. "Paranoid.

This mission has been one disaster after another and things keep going from bad to worse."

He sighed and ran a hand though his hair. "For all we know, this could have been an accident."

"Is that what you really think?" Chaney asked.

"No."

Chaney didn't either.

When Nakeisha stirred and awoke, the first thing she saw was Chaney. His feet were propped up on the bed she was in and he was leaning back against a wall. His eyes were closed and he looked decidedly uncomfortable. She couldn't hold back a smile at the sight.

The moment she sat up, Chaney's eyes snapped open. His feet hit the floor and he sat up with only the slightest of winces.

"You're awake! How do you feel?"

It took her a moment to decide. "I am feeling well. How long was I unconscious?"

"Almost seven hours," he said. He stood up. "How much do you remember?"

"I remember going to the dining hall for something to eat," she said hesitantly. "I shared a meal with Libby and Nigel and went back to my quarters. I remember feeling very strange, and attempting to go to the med-lab."

"You only made it as far as the door."

Her brow creased as she thought. "I remember nothing else until awakening just now. What happened to me?"

"You were poisoned," he said bluntly.

Her eyes widened in alarm. "Poisoned? With what and for what reason?"

He sat down on the edge of her bed. "Somehow you ingested a derivative of thanium. Nigel found traces of it in the F.P.U. and he's taking it apart for cleaning as we speak."

"So it was an accident."

He shook his head. "Not necessarily. There's also the possibility that someone was testing you."

"Testing me for what?"

"Apparently only a few races have a reaction as bad as yours to thanium . . ."

"The Old Races being among them?" she guessed.

"I'm afraid so."

"Someone was looking for confirmation I am not what I appear to be," she said slowly. This could be very dangerous for them all.

"That would be my guess," he said. "But we have no idea who."

"I seem to cause trouble no matter where I go," Nakeisha said unhappily.

"No, never think that!" he clasped one of her hands between his. "You bring joy, not trouble."

She smiled up at him. "Perhaps we bring each other joy. Is there a need for me to stay in the med-lab?"

"No, I was just waiting for you to wake up."

"Then perhaps you would be kind enough to escort me back to my quarters."

Chaney was silent as he walked Nakeisha back to her quarters, so silent in fact that she kept casting sidelong glances his way to make sure he was still beside her. When he hesitated at her door, she paused as well.

"Aren't you coming in?" she asked.

He looked at her gravely. "You've been through a lot," he said finally. "I should let you get some rest."

She was confused, had he changed his mind about her? After everything that had happened she couldn't blame him. Her mouth opened to protest and then she peered closer at him.

"After seven hours of rest, I don't believe I require any more." It was her turn to hesitate. "Unless you must report for duty?"

"I'm off duty for the next full cycle."

With the barest hint of a smile on her face, she opened the door and ushered him inside, stumbling slightly over the wine bottle and goblets on the floor. "What is this?"

Chaney flushed as he bent down to scoop them up. "I forgot about these. When I came to see you . . . that is, earlier . . . I thought . . . ." He stuttered to a halt, mortified. What was the matter with him?

Nakeisha found his embarrassment endearing. She took the bottle and goblets from him with a smile. "It was most thoughtful of you to bring them with you earlier. I fear I have little in the way of refreshment."

"The wine is from Soropo," he said, feeling the knot of discomfort in his chest loosen.

"Then I am twice honored," she said. "The wines of Soropo are both rare and legendary."

"Perhaps we should share a glass and you can judge for yourself," he suggested.

She broke the wax seal on the bottle and poured the dark red liquid into the two goblets. Handing him one, she took a sip from the other. Her eyes widened in surprise. "This is incredible!" It was tart, with a hint of sweetness, and seemed to evaporate on her tongue. The flavor made her think of cool, star-filled nights and hot desert days.

"It's made from the fruit of the *gourcat* plant that blooms only once every seven years."

Chaney seated himself on the sofa and she sat down beside him. Now that they were here, together, she found herself curiously tongue-tied. The silence stretched between them as they sipped their wine. It wasn't an uncomfortable silence, more one of anticipation.

Reaching up, she gently traced the markings on his cheek. "Did it hurt, when this was done to you?"

"That was the idea," he said gravely. "It was a rite of passage from boy to man."

"And you bore it without so much as flinching." It wasn't a question, but a statement of fact. In such a short time she'd learned him so well.

"To do otherwise would have brought great dishonor to my tribe."

Nakeisha set her empty goblet on a low table and moved closer, cupping his face between her hands. "Such bravery surely deserves a reward," she whispered, and without further hesitation kissed him.

He kissed her back, tentative at first, then more demanding as she melted against him. She tasted of the wine they shared and a sweetness that was all her own. His arms went around her and he gathered her closer. Her hands skimmed along his face and into his hair, which she loosened from its queue.

Pulling back slightly, she smiled up at him.

"What is it?"

"Since I first met you I've wondered what your hair would look like unconfined," she confessed.

"And what do you think?"

"I think you are most beautiful."

"How is it that you've never formed a bond with anyone?" he asked in wonder.

"I was waiting for you."

The sincerity in her eyes was his undoing. Chaney kissed her again, fiercely, possessively. Sweeping her up in his arms he carried her into the bed chamber, sitting down on the bed with her across his lap. Her arms were around him and she whimpered slightly as he broke off the kiss.

"Are you sure this is what you want?" he asked, even now not quite able to believe it.

"More than anything," she told him.

Chapter Seventeen

He had no more strength of will to argue, he didn't even know why he was trying to. He'd bedded other women; it was a natural biological function. But this time it was different, the woman was different. This time the woman was Nakeisha, and what they were about to do would change everything.

Though he knew her strength, he was very careful as he turned and laid her on the bed. She looked so fragile, eyes wide and luminous in her pale face, lips red and roughened by his kisses. She reached up to him, but instead of pulling him down, her hands went to the fastenings on his uniform.

Chaney couldn't hold back his smile. "Impatient are we?"

"Yes," she said, not stopping. "I do not know how long I can hold back the wind."

He realized that the air around them was profoundly still.

"Help me with this!" she demanded.

He leaned down to kiss her again and she momentarily forgot what she was doing. This time it was a
slow, leisurely kiss, an easy pressure of his lips against
hers. Nakeisha's protest was lost against his gentle as-
sault. Her hands slid up his chest to tangle in his hair
again. A smile curved his lips when he felt a whisper
of a breeze around them.

Nakeisha ached. Her skin, where Chaney touched
her, felt like it was on fire. It was well she was not a
fire elemental or they would have both gone up in
flames by now. She needed . . . she wasn't quite sure
what she needed, but she knew it wasn't this slow and
gentle torture.

Her hands loosened from his hair and moved
down to his shoulders to push him away. Her eyes
opened in shock when she felt, not the cloth of his
uniform, but warm, firm skin beneath her hands. She
pulled back in astonishment.

"How did you do that?" Somehow he'd divested
himself of his uniform while he'd been kissing her.

"Practice," he said smugly.

Practice with whom? There was a spike in the air
around them as momentary jealousy filled her. Ruth-
lessly she pushed the feeling aside. It did not matter.
What mattered was that he was here with her now.

"You are beautiful," she said in wonder, running
her hands over the hard, smooth planes of his chest.
His sun-kissed skin was warm under her touch,
twitching slightly as her caresses became bolder.

"You have me at an advantage," he said, catching her hands in his.

Wordlessly, she slipped out of his grasp and stood beside the bed. With a flick of her hand she undid her robe and it slithered downwards to pool around her feet. There was a faint flush to her pale skin, her breath caught as she allowed him to look his fill.

When he held out his hand, she rejoined him on the bed. The air around them swirled gently.

"You are a work of art," he said, running his hand down her breast, across her hip. She shivered in response, arching into his touch, returning his caresses with her own.

Their touches became firmer, more assured. The slight breeze surrounding them began to strengthen, hot and dry like the coming of a summer storm. Chaney caught the scent of the desert wind. He kissed a line up her throat, along her jaw, then captured her lips once more, tongues dueling intimately.

There was a vibration in the air, the heavy feeling of expectation. Nakeisha felt as though she was about to combust.

"Please," she begged, not even sure what she was begging for, her control of the wind slipping.

Chaney moved to cover her body with his own, then stopped, eyes widening in surprise as he felt the thin barrier.

"No, don't stop!"

Her arms tightened around him, pulling him closer. He plunged forward, capturing her soft cry in his mouth as the air around them exploded into a small whirlwind.

Chaney shifted slightly, drawing a sleepy protest from Nakeisha. At some point one of them had drawn a blanket over them, she was nestled securely in his arms beneath it. He buried his face in her hair, inhaling the fragrance of her perfume and the subtle scent that was uniquely Nakeisha.

"Why didn't you tell me?" he whispered against her sweat-dampened neck.

She sighed, and for a moment he thought she wasn't going to answer.

"I did not wish it to keep us from what we both wanted," she said at last.

"But such a gift—"

She freed one hand from under the covers to place her fingers against his lips to silence him.

"It was my gift to give. Would you undo what has been done?"

He struggled with his answer, but in the end was forced to tell the truth. "No, I would not."

"Good." She snuggled against him again.

Chaney relaxed. There was so much he wanted to say to her, but now was not the time. Now was the time to enjoy the feel of Nakeisha in his arms. If ever there was a time of contentment, this was it.

The crackling static of the ship's intercom made them both start. "Chaney, report to the bridge."

"*Thersta!*"

Chaney smiled at her vehement tone and kissed the top of her head before slipping out of the bed.

"It's just as well," he told her. "Nigel advised that you were to rest and I fear you would not get much of that were I to stay."

Nakeisha rolled over onto her side and propped herself up on one elbow. She watched silently as he dressed. Though making love with Chaney had been everything she dreamed of, the aftermath left much to be desired.

When he finished dressing, Chaney knelt beside the bed so he was eye level with her. He stared at her silently and then leaned in to kiss her, softly, gently.

"I'm sorry I have to go. I wish . . ."

"I'll keep your place warm."

"See that you do, woman," he said with mock severity. He kissed her one last time and reluctantly departed.

Though she'd been dozing in Chaney's arms, Nakeisha was too keyed up for sleep now. She sat up in bed and then grimaced at the state of her room. There was a wide circle of debris around the bed; vaguely she remembered losing control of her winds.

With a sigh she got up and started cleaning up the mess, imagining what E.Z. was going to have to say. It didn't matter. She was a grown woman and quite capable of making her own decisions. And for a short while she had been able to control her wind, so that, at least, was progress.

She was filled with a restless energy. When she finished with the bedroom, she took a long, leisurely bath and then went into the main area of her quarters to meditate. After an hour, she gave up meditation as a lost cause. How could she clear her mind when her body was still tingling from Chaney's touch?

It was then that she realized she still hadn't heard from E.Z. She frowned. This wasn't like him at all. Where did he go when he wasn't with her?

"E.Z.?" She asked tentatively. "Are you there?"

Worried now, she tried again, using her mind. *E.Z.?* It's safe to come out now. Chaney had to leave, so we're alone. E.Z.?

Closing her eyes, she searched with her mind but could find no trace of her friend and mentor.

"E.Z.? Where are you? Why won't you answer?"

With each passing minute, Nakeisha was growing more alarmed. She couldn't sense E.Z. at all, and their connection seemed more tenuous than ever. A shiver went up her spine.

Chapter Eighteen

The pleasant mood that had sustained Chaney throughout his duty on the bridge vanished the moment Nakeisha opened her door. She seemed distracted, troubled even. His heart sank further when she led him inside without a word.

He should have realized that there was no future for them, she was too far above him in station. It was obvious she'd changed her mind about what happened between them, not that he could blame her. The first words out of her mouth, however, were not what he expected.

"I fear I have lost my link to E.Z.," she said as she paced the length of the room.

"Who is E.Z.?"

She turned, surprised at the bewildered look on his face. "Oh, I—"

Smiling a little sheepishly, she took his unresisting hand and led him over to the sofa. Sitting down beside him, she said, "I am sorry, I forgot you do not know. E.Z. is–was–is my Ilezie companion. Do you recall I told you and the captain that I was *Illarie*, a vessel?"

"Yes, I remember."

"The ability to carry E.Z.'s essence within me is what makes me *Illarie*. But now I fear I have . . . lost him."

Her voice was trembling by the time she finished. Without even having to think, he gathered her into his arms.

"Has this ever happened before, to any of your people?"

"Not to my knowledge," she replied, voice muffled.

"I don't pretend to understand how you are able to be this, *Illarie*, but perhaps it was just his time to move on."

She shook her head and pulled back enough to look up at him. "That is not the way it works. Once a vessel is filled with an ovele, or soul, the only way to separate the two is through a ceremony that must take place on Ilezinea."

"What can we do?"

"I do not know," she whispered, resting her head on his chest again.

They sat like that for a long while. Finally Chaney asked, "Is there someone you could talk to about this, someone on your world perhaps?"

"That would prove . . . difficult, if not impossible. Communications with my world are limited to a handful of frequencies and I do not know which ones they are."

"Why wouldn't—oh. I take it E.Z. knew them?"

With a heavy sigh she shifted until she was sitting beside him again. "There was no reason to believe we would become separated. But in any case, I could not risk the chance of the signal being traced to Ardraci."

"Why would that be a problem?"

Nakeisha hesitated. "If we are to be together there are things you must know."

He placed a hand under her chin to raise her face up to his for a kiss. "Never doubt that I wish us to be together."

"I feel the same," she said softly.

"You saw what I was able to do on Temus, and again with the Deraidne ship. Imagine if someone was holding my family hostage, the damage I could be made to do."

"But surely you could defend yourselves . . ."

"Yes, up to a point. But only a small percentage of our population has enough power to make a difference in defense. This is one of the reasons we have avoided contact with outsiders. If our application to the Pan-Galactic Council is denied, the Ilezie will hide our world for all time."

Chaney frowned. "That seems a little extreme."

"These are extreme times. The Corporate Alliance and Sector Federation have offered obscene rewards for information leading to Ardraci."

"I think I can understand that," Chaney said slowly. "But surely, given the circumstances, you could risk contacting—"

Nakeisha was shaking her head before he finished. "Even if I could find a communications network that can reach that far, there would be no way of them receiving the message. No, there is only one thing we can do. We will have to contact the Ilezie."

"Contact the Ilezie." Captain Blake repeated when Chaney and Nakeisha sought him out to fill him in on this new development. One of the *eoflessi* sat on the captain's bar, already activated before he even opened the door. He had a feeling that only something important would have brought them to his quarters. He hated being right.

"It should be easy enough," he said.

"I do not expect it to be easy," Nakeisha replied. "But it must be done."

"We have a signal booster on our communications grid, the council paid for the upgrade when they commissioned us."

"It will not be enough," she told him apologetically. "There are only certain places from which one can contact the Ilezie easily. The Great Library was one of them, but I would not wish us to move backwards at this point."

"I agree," Blake said. "Where else can you communicate with them?"

"There are seven temples from which it is possible. I do not know if there are any near."

Chaney tapped into the navigational computer to bring up an image on the captain's monitor. Touching the screen he said, "This is where we are currently. The closest planet to us is Desthimea."

Nakeisha peered over his shoulder. "Can you show more of this sector?"

He made the necessary adjustment and the view pulled back.

"Is there some way to show details of each world? Things such as atmosphere and mineral content . . ."

The specifications of each of the planets appeared on a side bar on the screen.

"I am not sure . . ." Nakeisha hesitated. She gave a short laugh and shook her head ruefully. "If you only knew how new all this is to me."

"You're doing fine," Chaney assured her, smiling warmly.

The captain was not at all surprised to see her returning the navigator's smile before focusing on the task at hand. It would take a greater fool than he to miss the attraction between the pair.

"There," she pointed at the screen. "That one should suit our purposes."

"Anchyre?" Blake asked. He sighed. "Why am I not surprised that it's the one furthest away from our current position?"

"I am truly sorry, Captain. But the isolation of its position is part of what makes it a good choice."

"And you're sure you'll be able to contact the Ilezie from here?"

"No, Captain. I am not sure at all."

"Then—"

She held up a hand to stop his protest. "It is no easy thing for a human to contact the Ilezie without a conduit from one of the temples, even humans as closely associated with them as my people are. Certain preparations must be made, conditions must be met . . ."

"What kind of conditions?" Chaney asked, curious.

"Anchyre has a dry, arid atmosphere and an unusually high magnetic force at its poles."

"And strong wind patterns," Chaney added, checking the screen for details. "Is that a part of it too?"

"It is for me," she admitted. "For another the conditions would need to be quite different."

"Well, that settles it then," the captain said. "Chaney, I suggest you get to the bridge and lay in a course to Anchyre, while I work on the hard part of this little side trip."

"What part would that be?" Chaney asked.

"I'm the one that has to figure out a plausible explanation for our change of course."

Chapter Nineteen

"Where did you say you got this tip?" Nigel asked, staring at the view screen as the scanner panned across the desolate landscape below them.

Chaney's lips twitched at the look of dismay on the doctor's face. There was not much to see. Anchyre was mostly barren rock, dusty plains, and windswept sand dunes. The planet depended on extensive mining operations to keep it going, it was rich in precious metals and gem stones.

"I got it in the usual way," the captain said evasively. The captain announced to the crew that a message had come from the Council giving them a new lead on their assignment. Since this had been happening on a regular basis, no one questioned it. And since their mission was supposedly a secret he led them to believe that Nakeisha was told they were tracking the lead on an independent trading agreement for a large trade cartel.

"I suggest we work in pairs, Nigel and Libby, Chaney and Nakeisha, and I'll take Vida with me."

"It's not as bad as it looks," Chaney said, clapping the doctor on the back.

"Of course you'd think so, being a desert dweller yourself. But some of us enjoy more civilized pursuits."

"I hear the tavern dancers are very . . . limber."

"Really?" the doctor brightened marginally. "Taverns are a good place to find information," he said thoughtfully.

The captain rolled his eyes while Chaney grinned, both behind Nigel's back.

The doctor took one last look at the view screen and then turned to leave. "It can't be any worse than Tersic."

"Do you think it's wise to pair Libby with Nigel?" Chaney asked as the door slid shut.

Blake sighed. "Probably not, but we do need to make this look like a legitimate fact-finding mission."

A chime sounded, indicating an incoming message.

"It's about time," Chaney muttered.

"Blake here," the captain said, switching on the communications.

"Captain Blake," the Anchryean official acknowledged. He was a short, round man with a bald head that gleamed under the lights in his office. His face seemed to be set in a permanent scowl.

"We have reviewed your petition to land and have decided to honor your request. I will transmit the landing coordinates. Do not disembark until a port official has contacted you."

"Thank you," the captain said. "I–"

He stopped talking when the view went black.

"Friendly sort, isn't he?" Chaney said.

"Let's hope the citizens are friendlier. I'd hate to have to spend all my time in a tavern with Libby and Nigel."

Chaney laughed, then took his leave to tell Nakeisha they'd been given permission to land.

"Not much to look at, is it?" Nakeisha asked as they disembarked.

Up close the landscape was even more desolate. A pale sun shone high in the grey sky. The grey extended down to the horizon, before changing slightly in hue before spreading out over the landscape.

There was very little vegetation to be seen, just sparse grass and the odd, leafless tree. The city of Galmer was small by most standards, but all it was really needed for was as a port of call for the shipping of ore. The population swelled twice a year when the shifts changed at the mines, and a tent city surrounded the city proper.

The official that met them was tall and thin, but also bald and scowling.

"You will not find much in the way of entertainment, save for the taverns, as this is mid-shift. You will each wear one of these tracking devices." He handed out wristbands. "This is the law. If your wristband begins to glow, take cover immediately. It means that there's a dust storm coming. It can scour the skin off a man in a matter of minutes. We have a force dome that protects the city, venture beyond the city limits at your own risk. Welcome to Anchyre."

Speech finished, he turned on his heal and left.

"Well, that was welcoming, wasn't it?" Nigel said.

"All right everyone," the captain said. "You've got your assignments, I suggest we get to work."

"Aye, captain," the others chorused. They paired off and vanished into the city.

Nakeisha could not shake a feeling of impending doom. It had been a niggling sensation since she first became aware of E.Z.'s absence, growing steadily worse the longer he was gone. As she waited for Chaney to hire an air-car, the feeling became almost unbearably urgent. A small breeze swirled around her.

"Is there a problem?" she asked, interrupting the negotiations.

From the tightness of Chaney's face he appeared to be holding onto his temper by a thread. "This person does not wish to rent us an air-car."

"Good sir, good lady, these vehicles are my only livelihood. The loss of even one . . ." he spread his hands wide in a helpless gesture. "It is too dangerous to take one beyond the city's protection grid. What if something should happen?"

"I'm an experienced pilot, I won't let anything happen."

"This is the storm season. It is too risky to travel far from the city. Even the mine workers do not come."

"We're willing to take the risk!"

"Not with my air-car!"

The two men glared at each other.

"You are worried for your air-car, and rightly so," Nakeisha said. "Should you lose it, you would lose your livelihood, yes?"

"That is correct."

"Then perhaps this will help alleviate some of your fears." She handed him a small, clear blue gem.

The native held it up so the sun shone through it. "Very nice, yes. Very nice indeed. "

He hesitated, the gem still clutched in his hand. "I do not magnify the danger outside of the city at this time of year. The air-car will not protect you from the wind storms."

"Do not fear for us, my friend," Nakeisha said gently, laying a hand on his shoulder. "We have nothing to fear from the wind."

Reluctantly, the merchant parted with the air-car. Though he said nothing further, they could see he was still filled with misgivings. He followed them to the car and laid a restraining hand on Chaney's arm as he settled into his seat.

"If a storm does arise, do not head for the rock formations, search for lower ground. It could be your only hope."

"Thank you," Chaney said, "We'll do that."

The merchant watched as they sped from the city and shrugged philosophically. He'd done what he could. The rest was up to the gods. Opening his clenched fist, he grinned. With a gem such as this he could buy a dozen air-cars. Or maybe even passage off this rock.

The city was far behind them before Nakeisha requested a stop. Chaney brought the air-car to a rest in the shadow of a cluster of giant boulders. The rocks were grey, as was the fine dust covering them. There was nothing alive that he could see, not birds, nor reptiles, nor even insects. It was barren and lifeless.

Where Tersic had some similarities to his home world, this planet had none. It was no wonder the miners only stayed for six month work furloughs. It was too depressing. Even the space port was subdued.

"We need to adjust our course," Nakeisha said.

He helped her down from her perch atop one of the boulders where she'd gone to meditate. She dusted her grey robe off, then stopped with a short laugh.

"What is it?"

"I just realized that I appear to color coordinate with this world."

Chaney looked at her and grinned. Her robe was exactly the same color as the rock and sand. "You do blend in rather well."

He pulled her over to him and kissed her on the forehead. "I think you'd blend in well no matter what planet you were on."

"I–" she sighed and allowed herself to lean against him for a moment. "If I may be so bold, I think it is we who blend well together."

His arms tightened slightly. "I think you are right."

Reluctantly she pulled away. "We must continue. I fear we are growing short of time."

"Your wish is my command," he said. "Just point the way."

Chapter Twenty

"You're sure this is the right place?" Chaney asked dubiously. They'd been traveling for hours, and as far as he was concerned, the landscape hadn't changed much. This pile of rocks looked the same as the last five they'd checked out.

"Yes," Nakeisha said with more assurance than she felt.

She had paced a circuit around the rocks and returned to where the air-car was resting. The sense of doom she'd been feeling earlier had grown to something near panic. At this point she wasn't sure of anything, save that whatever they were going to do must be done quickly.

"So what now?"

"Now, I will need my bag."

Chaney slid down off the nose of the air-car where he'd been sitting and reached into the back for Nakeisha's bag. She took it from him absently, already focused on the task ahead. He touched her arm, making her pause.

"Are you sure about this?" Though his people were known for their stoicism, Chaney felt anything but that where Nakeisha was concerned.

"Am I sure this is the right place? Of the place we have searched, this is the most promising."

"I meant are you sure this is a good idea. I've heard stories . . ."

"I, too, have heard tales. I have also witnessed the results of how unforgiving the Ilezie can be. But I have little choice in the matter."

"Is this dangerous for you?" he asked suddenly.

"Yes. No! I—" Nakeisha sighed. "Not in the way you might think. I will be in no physical danger."

"But . . ." he prodded.

"But there is a danger of losing my 'self' in this attempt, that which is unique to me."

Chaney gathered her in his arms and held her close. "I have only just found you. I do not wish to lose you."

Tears pricked at the corners of her eyes. "Nor I, you," she admitted. "But I have to find out what happened to E.Z."

"I know. I just wish there was another way."

He loosened his hold and she pulled back just enough to look up at him. Resting one slender palm on his cheek she confessed, "I will be fine."

Chaney answered her with a kiss. If there was a hint of desperation to it, neither of them paid attention. Nakeisha's arms stole around his neck as she pressed closer.

Breaking off with a gasp, she said, "I think you are trying to distract me."

"Is it working?" he asked with a grin.

She slapped him playfully on the arm. "Yes. Now stop it."

Stretching upwards, she gave him one last kiss. Chaney reluctantly let her go. Resolutely she turned back to the task at hand.

Surveying the boulders with a critical eye, she chose one with a somewhat flattened surface. With little effort she climbed to the top. A quick glance showed Chaney watching her from below, clearly not happy with what she was about to do but trusting her to do it anyway. It amazed her that they had found each other over so great a distance.

"Would you like a cushion?"

She appreciated his attempt at levity. "It is not so bad. There is a layer of sand up here." Kneeling down, she reached into her bag.

He resumed his perch on the vehicle, watching as she pulled four balls from the bag, similar to the *eoflessi*, but smaller in size. She positioned them carefully on the rock and then sat back on her heels, arms outstretched and eyes closed.

Chaney sat cross-legged on the nose of the air-car, resigned to a lengthy wait. While another man might have started to fidget, he held as still as Nakeisha. The air held a silence of expectation that was unnerving. His eyes were in continuous motion, checking the horizon, the sky, Nakeisha, and back again.

The days were longer here than on Soropo and he had only a mild sense of time passing. The sun was not the bright one he was used to, the shadows were too faint to make an accurate judgment. He would be glad to leave this world behind. The wind, normally a mild presence on Anchyre, was starting to pick up. It was making him more uneasy, perhaps they should have taken the vendor's warnings a little more seriously.

"Any luck?" he called up to Nakeisha.

She was about to answer when she suddenly stiffened, head thrown back. Contact.

Chaney slid off the air-car and took a step towards her.

Do not touch her, a voice said.

Chaney froze, then darted a look around him. "Who—" he turned in a full circle, drawing his sidearm. "All right, whoever you are, show yourself."

Be at ease, tribesman. I mean no harm.

"Where are you?" Chaney demanded.

I am within you.

"That's not possible!"

The voice was laced with humor. *All things are possible my friend.*

"Who are you?"

My name is Elea'zareganeherneinar. But you can call me E.Z.

Nakeisha could feel the power building as she tapped into the wind. It was like having a river of light pour through her. If she could have screamed, she would have. She heard Chaney speak, but was unable to understand him. Her world narrowed to the power of Anchyre's wind.

This was nothing like the minor winds of her home world; it was so much more than the solar winds she used to destroy the Deraidne ship. She'd never felt anything like it before. It was almost too much.

The power continued to pour into her. It burned, a whirling maelstrom inside of her. She felt her control start to slip and desperately fought to strengthen her focus. If this much power escaped it would kill not only her and Chaney, but do significant damage to the planet as well.

Just when she thought she might split at the seams from it, it burst forth in an incandescent stream towards the Ilezie home world. She felt it stretch, and thin, and finally, it was caught.

Who seeks an audience with the Ilezie? The booming voice was loud in her head.

I am Nakeisha, of the Windsinger clan.

You are known to us, the voice continued in a more reason-able volume.

Why have you contacted us? Where is your mentor?

Forgive me, great one. My mentor is gone.

Gone? What mean you?

Not sparing herself in the least, Nakeisha explained about their capture by the T'tenet, E.Z.'s death, her becoming a filled vessel, and finally, her sense of E.Z.'s presence vanishing.

Give me your thoughts, the voice demanded.

If Nakeisha had been capable of movement, she'd have shivered. This was the most dangerous part of speaking with the Ilezie, the part she dreaded.

Chapter Twenty-One

The wind continued to pick up steadily but the landing site was an oasis in the coming storm. Though the wind flowed in a circle around it, it barely raised the dust within it.

"E.Z." Chaney repeated. "E.Z.? Nakeisha's E.Z.?"

Yes, tribesman. The voice seemed almost amused.

"In the name of all that's holy, what are you doing in my head? I'm no vessel!"

No, indeed you are not, E.Z. said. *I am sorry, but explanations will have to wait until the testing is complete.*

Chaney stared up to where Nakeisha knelt on the rock, frozen in place. It must have been a trick of the light, but she seemed almost to glow.

"What's happening?" Chaney's fists were clenched in frustration. He badly wanted to hit something. "What are you doing to her?"

Each candidate must be tested in a way that is unique to them.

"Nakeisha never mentioned any kind of a test. And why didn't you speak up sooner? You must have known how worried she is."

So many questions, you and she have much in common in that regard.

"Some answers would be nice."

Chaney could swear he felt a sigh in his head. *She did not mention the test because she did not know of it. None of the candidates know. I did not speak sooner because it was part of the test. Yes, I knew she was worried, and I do regret it, but it was necessary.*

"Will she be all right?"

There was a pronounced hesitation before E.Z. answered. *She is stronger than she knows. That will work in her favor.*

Chaney didn't like the sound of that at all.

It was a distinctly unpleasant feeling, like a ghostly hand sifting through her mind. When the connection between her and the Ilezie seemed to thin, Nakeisha drew more energy from around her. It was chancy, because of the volatile nature of Anchyre's weather patterns, but losing the connection was out of the question.

She could feel the sweat beading up on her face, trickling down her neck and between her breasts. Or maybe it was tears as the unpleasant feeling became a painful one. Frozen in place, Nakeisha could not even brush the moisture away.

Memories flooded her. The first time she manifested a wind, and all the times after that. The training she underwent; her strengths and weaknesses. Next came more recent memories, her torture at the hands of the T'tenet, the death of E.Z., her retaliation on Temus.

Then the memory of the Deraidne ship, and how she'd used the solar wind to destroy it. Every use of her gift, whether conscious or unconscious, was weighed against her. At last the phantom hand released her.

Your control is less than absolute the voice informed her.

I am sorry, I–

It is of little consequence.

But I–

You did well in the altercation with the T'tenet.

Thank you, I–

Your unconscious control is better.

What about–

Tell your mentor that you are not the One.

With that the contact was broken. The moment the Ilezie withdrew from her mind, Nakeisha's paralysis ended. She slumped forward and the wind surged inwards, then back again as she reasserted her control over it. Her eyes widened as she became aware of just how strong the wind had become.

Now you may go to her, E.Z. whispered in Chaney's mind.

Chaney lost no time in climbing the rock.

"Are you all right?" he asked, kneeling carefully beside her. He had to yell to be heard over the sound of the wind.

"I think so, yes," Nakeisha said, somewhat surprised.

"You mean you had doubts?" Chaney asked, anger building again at the thought of her taking what turned out to be such an unnecessary risk.

She was in no danger. We have the best interests of her people at heart.

"I'm sorry," Nakeisha yelled over the increasing volume of the wind. "I grew up hearing stories of those who tried, but failed to contact the Ilezie. They lost control of their elements and were swept away. I didn't want to worry you , but it had to be done."

Is this true?

Only once, to my knowledge, and the man was unstable to begin with.

"I understand," he said, putting his arms around her and pulling her into a hug . "Just don't do it again."

She snuggled closer to his warmth. "It was all for nothing, they riffled through my mind but in the end told me nothing of what happened to E.Z."

Chaney opened his mouth, but shut it again. *And just how am I going to explain this?* he asked E.Z. angrily.

Somehow he was not surprised when there was no answer.

"I know what happened to E.Z."

Nakeisha pulled back to look at him. "How could you know?"

"Because E.Z. himself told me."

She stared at him in astonishment.

"Somehow he ended up in my head. He only revealed himself after you made contact with the Ilezie."

"That's impossible, you're no vessel!"

Chaney gave a snort of laughter. "That's what I told him."

"How is this possible?"

Always so many questions. Why can you humans not just accept what is?

After relaying what E.Z. said, Chaney asked, "How did you move from her mind to mine without us knowing?"

With the Ilezie, all things are possible. It was a simple matter to transfer my consciousness while you and she were joined.

Chaney relayed what E.Z. said.

The wind surrounding the rock began to spin faster as Nakeisha's temper flared. "Are my people nothing but toys for the Ilezie to manipulate?"

That is an unworthy question.

"Then tell us why you felt it necessary to put Nakeisha through all this," Chaney asked.

Each Ardraci must undergo a testing journey, it has been that way for generations. To know of this before hand would taint the test.

"The Ilezie I spoke with said to tell you I was not "the one". What did he mean?" Nakeisha asked when Chaney passed on what E.Z. said.

A very few are tested to see if they are the One that was foretold in ages past. The Redeemer. The One who will be savior to us all.

"So everything Nakeisha's been through has been part of some test and you've determined she's not this Redeemer person. So now what?"

Now what?

"Now what?" Nakeisha echoed.

"Where do we go from here?"

Chapter Twenty-Two

What do we do now? Chaney repeated in his mind when E.Z. failed to answer right away.

E.Z. gave a mental shrug. *Now you two will have to wait out the storm before making your way back to the city.*

Chaney repeated what he said to Nakeisha.

"But, they said I was not the One."

She is not the Redeemer, E.Z. corrected. *But she still has an appointment to keep with the Council.*

"But didn't I fail my test? What about my lack of control?"

Tell her to open her eyes, E.Z. said.

Chaney relayed the message, then added, "Was he this annoying when he was corporeal?"

"Always," Nakeisha said absently, looking around them. Her eyes widened suddenly. "Chaney, look!"

It was like being in the eye of a hurricane. The wind screamed as it whirled around them, creating a vortex of sand and debris but never coming within more than a few feet of the boulders. It was as though an invisible hand was holding it back.

Is she doing that, he asked silently.

Indeed she is. She passed her test. She has full control of her element.

Then why is it still so windy?

She needed the power of the storm to contact the Ilezie. The storm she raised, however, is too powerful to direct at a target, it needs to dissipate naturally.

Will this change her?

Only in that she no longer needs to use her own energy to raise the wind.

"I've never felt such a connection to the wind before," Nakeisha said.

Chaney tightened his arms around her. "You truly are an elemental now."

And now children, I must leave you for a time.

"What do you mean?"

It is time for me to return to the Ilezie, but never fear, we will meet again before the Council.

"Wait a minute," Chaney said. "You can't just—"

Take care of each other, E.Z. said, and then his presence vanished.

Startled at the turn of events, Chaney repeated what E.Z. said. Nakeisha took the news quite calmly.

"While the Ilezie were rifling through my mind I also learned a few things about them," she admitted. "I believe E.Z. only stayed with me to help me with my element, and that he is returning to his home world to acquire a new body."

"The Ilezie can do that?"

"You doubt it, having housed his consciousness yourself?" she asked with a smile.

"After this, I think I'll believe anything where the Ilezie are concerned."

"We will have to come up with a plausible story about how we survived the storm," Nakeisha said after a few minutes.

"Can you tell how much longer it's going to last?"

She closed her eyes briefly. "It will be several hours before it will be at a low enough ebb that I can safely help it dissipate."

"Several hours?" he asked, lips close to her ear. "I was going to suggest we take shelter in the ship, but I think it's much more comfortable up here."

Turning in his arms, she brushed her lips against his. "However will we pass the time?"

"I'll think of something," he promised, lowering her to the blanket.

It was like being in a world where it was just the two of them. The wind and debris made a solid barrier against the outside. No one, and nothing, could get in. So much had happened in so short a time. More than anything, Chaney wished he was able to tell Nakeisha what was in his heart, but the noise from the storm made speech almost impossible.

He shook out the blanket she'd brought up with her but hadn't used and laid it on the sand filled hollow in the rock. No bed had ever looked more inviting, especially with Nakeisha on it. Smiling, she leaned back on her elbows and motioned for him to join her.

The hollows were gone from her face, she'd gained some much needed weight over the last few weeks. She had a beauty not only of face and form but of spirit as well. It was her spirit, more than anything else that had captured him. That same spirit was shining through her eyes. Perhaps words between them were not needed.

She lay passive as he undressed her slowly and watched with a heavy-lidded gaze as he removed his own clothing. At first he did nothing more than look at her, lying in front of him like an offering to the gods. Then, unable to help himself, he reached out and touched her.

Static electricity arced between them. He jerked his hand back then tried again. His eyes widened as he left a trail of sparks behind. There was a tingling sensation, but no pain, just the flickers of blue-white light. Chaney ran a single finger along her jaw, then down her throat, mesmerized by it.

He drew the symbol for joy between her breasts and as it faded skimmed his finger over one dusky nipple. Her mouth opened in a cry he was unable to hear as she arched into his touch. Again he stroked her breast, filling his hand with its silken weight, running his thumb over the taut peak. Leaning down he captured her mouth in a kiss.

Even their kiss was charged with electricity, centered where their lips met then spreading outwards. Lines of light writhed wherever their skin touched, leaving a trail of effervescence. Chaney had intended to take it slowly, take her slowly, but her hands were on him as well and he was lost to the sensation.

He stroked her breast, skimming his hand downwards along her ribs, across her flat belly. Quivering from his touch and needing to touch back, Nakeisha ran her hands over his chest, raking his flat male nipples lightly with her nails, fascinated by the ensuing sparks and by the way his muscles jumped and twitched under her hand.

His hand traveled lower, caressing her hip, stroking the soft flesh of her thigh. The energy coursing through them made even the slightest touch almost too pleasurable to bear. Need surged through her, pooling low in her groin. She felt, rather than heard him cry out as she wrapped one slender hand around his hard length, not even stroking, just holding him prisoner, needing that connection.

It was as though she had no control over her actions. She wanted to take her time, to give and receive pleasure, but she ached with an emptiness only Chaney could fill. She pulled him downwards, lifting her hips to meet him halfway. The feel of him, hot and hard, filling her, gave her only a momentary respite. It wasn't enough. It might never be enough.

The energy crawled over their skin, enveloping them, almost too intense. The air around them sizzled with primal power. He surged into her and she rose to meet him, wrapping her legs around his waist. She urged him on without words, harder, faster.

It was like a charge building up between them. They couldn't seem to get close enough. Harder, faster. Their mutual cry of pleasure was lost in an explosion of blue white light.

Chapter Twenty-Three

Nakeisha was the first to awaken. Chaney lay half-draped over her, his arm resting on her stomach, his legs twined with hers. The wind had lessened considerably. Reaching out easily with her mind, she slowed its speed further and nudged the storm gently away from them.

Chaney groaned, and stirred. He shifted, taking most of his weight with him, and opened his eyes. For a moment he looked confused, then concern replaced the confusion and he tenderly stroked her face.

"Are you all right?"

She smiled. "I am fine."

Chaney managed to sit up and helped her up as well. He winced as he saw the bruises on her, and gently touched them.

"I hurt you!"

"I am fine," she insisted. To prove it, she pulled his head down for a kiss. "We were not ourselves."

"What happened?"

"I do not know," she said. "I have never heard of an experience like it."

She moved closer and laid her hand on his chest. "The energy seems to have dissipated."

"I'd be happier knowing what caused it in the first place. This is a fine time for E.Z. to have deserted us."

Sighing, she rested her head on his shoulder. He put his arm around her and kissed the top of her head, then resolutely moved away.

"We should get back to the city."

"Are you sure I can't change your mind?" she asked, running her finger down the centre of his chest.

He caught her hand before it could go any lower and kissed her knuckles. "Absolutely you could change my mind, but I don't think I want to take the chance of the energy taking control of us again."

"I suppose you're right," she said with resignation.

"Besides," he said with a grin, "I hear there are nice, soft, beds in the city."

They dressed and then Chaney helped her down off the boulder. "I'd better check on the air-car."

Nakeisha took a moment to admire the view as he walked away before following.

"Oh, no!"

The area around the air-car was scoured clean by the wind, but even her inexperienced eye could tell the vehicle itself was damaged beyond repair.

"What are we going to do?" she asked.

Chaney was checking inside the craft for anything salvageable. The storm had pretty much stripped it bare.

He made a sound of disgust. "I left my communicator in here, but it's long gone now." He jumped back down. "It's getting late. They probably won't be able to send a search team out until the morning. Looks like we're stuck here for the night."

They sat side by side with their backs to the boulder and watched the sun set. As sunsets went it wasn't spectacular, just the glowing orb of the sun sinking slowly below the horizon. Nakeisha shivered and Chaney put his arm around her shoulders.

"Are you cold?" he asked, pulling her closer.

"No, it's just that this is such a desolate world," she said. "I would not like to have to make my home here."

"My people call worlds like this *giesthenis*, a dead world."

Nakeisha looked around them, at the grey landscape in the dying light. There was no plant life, no birds or animals, not even any reptiles or insects. If it were not for the sighing of the wind there would be no sound either. She suppressed another shiver.

"There may not be any wood for a fire," she said with determined cheerfulness, "But at least we will not go hungry."

"How do you figure that?"

"I have dried rations with me."

He grinned as she reached for her bag.

"Not that I'm complaining, but how did you know to bring rations with you?"

"When I work with the wind I am used to expending a lot of personal energy, which needs to be replaced as quickly as possible."

"And now that you've learned control, you're using the wind's energy and not your own," Chaney said, taking the ration bar she offered him.

He took a bite and chewed thoughtfully. "That's why you fainted on the bridge, you used up too much energy pushing the Deraidne ship away."

She didn't answer but the animation left her face.

"Stop that," he told her.

"Stop what?" she asked, not looking at him.

He put a hand under her chin and gently turned her face until she was looking at him. "It was not your fault. You had no way of knowing they were about to fire."

"In my mind I know this, but in my heart?" she sighed and leaned against him. "It is a terrible thing to know you are responsible for the loss of so many lives."

He put his arms around her and just held her, giving what comfort he could. Though he firmly believed her guilt was misplaced it was something she'd have to deal with on her own. After a few minutes she pulled away.

"I do not fancy sleeping on this hard packed earth tonight," she said. "I think we would be more comfortable on the bed of sand on the boulder."

"I think you're right," Chaney agreed, helping her up.

It was almost too dark to see by the time they settled themselves on the sand-filled hollow. Nakeisha lay with her head pillowed on Chaney's shoulder. Together they watched the stars appear, then the moons of Anchyre started their journey across the night sky.

"Do you know the story of the moons?" Chaney asked.

"They have a story?"

"The large one is called Kandor and the small one is Shinandu. Early in its history, Anchyre was ruled by a powerful warlord in the North and an equally powerful queen in the South."

"Their names wouldn't happen to be Kandor and Shinandu would they?"

"Yes. Now don't interrupt. The two were desperately in love, but a curse kept them apart."

"A curse?"

"It was believed that should Kandor and Shinandu ever come together, a disaster of epic proportions would befall Anchyre."

"What happened?"

"They may have been rulers, but they were only human after all, and eventually Kandor could stand it no longer and went to his beloved in the dark of night. She tried to resist, but was unable to withstand his charm. Their joining caused a cataclysmic explosion that blew them into the sky and caused Anchyre to become *giesthenis*."

"You made that up," Nakeisha accused, raising her head slightly to look at him.

"See for yourself," Chaney said. "Every night since, Kandor has chased Shinandu across the sky. It's said if he ever catches her, Anchyre will be restored to its former glory."

"It's a lovely story," she said, laying her head back down. "I hope some day Kandor catches Shinandu." She yawned and made herself more comfortable.

"Look," Chaney pointed. "A shooting star. My people believe them to be good omens."

"Hmm?" she murmured sleepily. "Mine make wishes on them."

"What did you wish for, Nakeisha?" he asked softly.

There was no answer. He turned his head to look at her and her eyes were closed. The day had finally caught up to her and she was asleep. With a contented sigh, Chaney, too, closed his eyes and went to sleep.

Chapter Twenty-Four

When Nakeisha awoke, it was to find Chaney, propped up on one elbow, watching her.

"Good morning," she said, stretching. "What is it that has you looking so serious?"

"I was thinking how much I would like to awaken every morning with you beside me."

She sat up and regarded him somberly for a moment. Whatever she saw must have reassured her because her expression softened and she reached over to lay her palm on his cheek. "Chaney, I—"

The rest of what she'd been about to say was lost in the sound of an approaching engine. Nakeisha sighed quietly, hand dropping as Chaney focused his attention on the air-car bearing down on their position.

"Looks like we're about to be rescued," he said, helping her up.

"Indeed."

By the time they climbed down from the rock, the air-car was parked beside the shell of their own vehicle.

"You'll have to make sure you get your fair share of the bet Cap made," Vida called to them as she opened the door.

"What bet is that?" Chaney asked.

"The townsfolk didn't think you two had a prayer out here during the storm, but he told them you were desert born and knew a few tricks about surviving."

She eyed them curiously. "I have to admit, even I had my doubts. The storm was so bad it knocked out the town's communications grid. Are you two all right?"

"We are fine," Nakeisha told her. "A little stiff from sleeping on the ground, but we took no harm from the storm."

"How did you find us so quickly?" Chaney asked.

Vida held up her arm to display the shining metal around her wrist. "I just tracked the wrist bands the officials at the space port made us wear. That and the fact you two are pretty much the only life signs registering out here."

Chaney could see she was burning with questions, but she kept them to herself. It was harder for her to hold back her surprise when he didn't insist on piloting them back to the spaceport. Normally he didn't allow anyone else in the pilot's seat. But then normally he didn't have Nakeisha curled beside him on the wide passenger seat. Vida raised an eyebrow but said nothing. Instead she sent a signal to the Burning Comet to let Cap know she'd found them.

Frowning, she tried sending the signal again.

"What's the matter?" Chaney asked.

"I can't raise the Comet."

"Did you not say the communications grid was not working? Perhaps the Comet's communications were affected by the storm as well," Nakeisha suggested.

"It's possible," Vida said, "But unlikely. They were working when I left."

"The Comet weathered the storm all right?" Chaney asked.

"The space port is covered by a protection grid just like the one the town has. We're only a few miles out now, we should be able to contact them."

"I do not like this," Nakeisha said.

"Nor do I," Chaney agreed. "But there's not much we can do about it. It's probably just a minor glitch in the system."

It wasn't long before they were back in the town, parking the air-car in its space in the rental lot. Vida was surprised the owner didn't come rushing out to lodge a protest over her taking one of his precious air-cars beyond the town limits.

"We're supposed to meet back at the Comet," she said, looking around carefully. The streets were empty, there wasn't even so much as a single person around. The houses and businesses were closed as well.

"It looks deserted," Nakeisha said as they made their way towards the space port. "Is this because of the storm?"

"I don't know," Vida replied. "It's possible."

"I'm getting a twitchy feeling," Chaney said. "Something's not right."

They entered the space port and stopped dead at the sight of an Alliance cruiser looming over the Burning Comet in the landing area. Before they were able to do anything else, they heard the sound of weapons being drawn behind them.

Chaney automatically moved closer to Nakeisha as they were quickly surrounded by Alliance troops. She tensed, as though prepared to fight, and he shook his head slightly at her. There were too many of them, and they were too well armed. Hopefully an opportunity to escape would present itself later.

He and Vida were divested of their weapons and then to his surprise they were herded away from the space port.

"Where are you taking us?" he demanded.

"No talking."

Nakeisha's brow furrowed in concentration. She'd felt a connection with Chaney almost from the beginning. But since yesterday, when they made love out in the desert, the connection had intensified. It was almost as though she could hear his thoughts. She tried to focus, narrowing her thoughts and reaching out with her mind.

They were taken to a large tavern the Alliance had taken over for their head quarters. Most of the tables and chairs had been removed, except for one close to the bar. The bar itself had been stripped of every bottle of liquor. The officer in charge was sitting at the table reading a report and didn't acknowledge their presence until he was finished.

"Which one of you is the Ardraci?" he barked, looking up at last.

"I am," Nakeisha replied, in a clear, steady voice.

He studied her from across the table. Chaney tensed at the look on the man's face. There was nothing sexual about it. He examined her impersonally, like she was a bug under a microscope. There was a distinct lack of compassion that Chaney found even more chilling.

"You don't look like much," the officer said at last. "You've led us on a merry chase, Ardraci. I hope for your sake it's been worth it."

She made no reply.

He studied her a moment longer. "Take those two," he nodded at Chaney and Vida, "and put them with the others."

Chaney resisted, unwilling to leave Nakeisha but this time it was she who shook her head slightly at him. *I will be all right,* she whispered in his mind.

His eyes widened slightly. They locked eyes for an instant. She gave a quick nod, and he allowed himself to be led away.

He and Vida were taken to a room at the back of the tavern and were given a shove to propel them through the door, which was locked behind them. Judging by the empty barrels and single cot, the room had probably been used as a store room. Unfortunately it seemed as well constructed as the rest of the tavern, a solid structure of local stone.

Libby and Captain Blake were already inside, Libby sitting cross-legged on the cot and the captain pacing back and forth.

"Are you two all right?" Blake asked.

"As well as can be expected," Chaney said. "What happened?"

Vida glanced around the room. "Nigel," she said succinctly.

"I'm afraid so," the captain admitted. "Just after you left to find Chaney and Nakeisha, Libby and I went to the bar leaving Nigel to monitor communications. The Alliance ship landed before we even knew it was there. He must have disabled the proximity alarm days ago for it to go undetected so long."

Chaney cursed in his own language.

"I'm almost afraid to ask what they want with Nakeisha," Vida said. "She is at the heart of the secret mission we've been on for the Council, is she not?"

"This can't be good for her," Libby chimed in. "Considering the shape she was in when we first found her."

Blake sighed. "You're right, both of you. Nakeisha is to represent her planet before the council and the Alliance has a vested interest to make sure that doesn't happen."

"So why don't they just kill her?" Vida asked. She shot a quick look at Chaney as he made a noise. "Sorry, but it just seems like they're going to a lot of trouble for someone they just want to get rid of."

"They need her alive to learn the location of her home world," he said. Rage and despair filled him as remembered the list of what had been done to her the last time the Alliance got their hands on her. There was no reason to believe they wouldn't treat her the same way this time, or worse. It was a miracle she'd survived once, there was no way she could survive that kind of torture again.

Libby shivered. "This really doesn't bode well for the poor girl."

Chapter Twenty-Five

Chaney paced back and forth within the confines of the small room, unable to keep still. Vida and Libby sat side by side on the cot, while Captain Blake perched on one of the empty barrels. They'd been in the room less than an hour, but it felt like an eternity to Chaney. The thought of what the Alliance could be doing right now to Nakeisha was more than he could bear.

"Will you sit down?" Blake asked in exasperation. He reached down and snagged another barrel, setting it upright.

There was a hesitation in the navigator's steps and then with a sigh he sat down. "We have to start planning our escape," he said.

"I'm open to suggestions," Blake said. "The four of us against a cruiser full of Alliance troops. It should be simple enough."

"As long as we breathe there is always hope," Vida said.

The others looked at her in surprise.

She shrugged. "It's what my grandmother always said, and she was a very wise woman."

Chaney opened his mouth to respond, then froze. *Chaney,* the voice whispered through his mind.

"Nakeisha?"

"What about Nakeisha?" Blake asked, puzzled.

Chaney held up a hand for silence. *Is that really you?*

Yes, it is I. They have confined me in another room.

How are you able to speak into my mind?

It is not unheard of for mated Ardraci to be able to speak mind to mind.

I'm not Ardraci. Wait—did you say mated?

There was a shy, uncertainty to her thoughts now. *Yes, I . . . I am sorry if this is not what you wished for.*

No! Never think that! He tried to project love and reassurance through the mind link but had no way of knowing if he succeeded. *I do not understand how it happened without us knowing, but I am glad that it did.*

I think . . . the energy surge we experienced. It did something to us, changed us.

Changed us how?

I do not know. But I feel a connection. Not just with you, but with Anchyre itself.

Are you all right? Did they harm you?

I am fine, she assured him. *They are waiting for someone of importance to arrive before questioning me.*

I don't like the sound of that, he told her.

Nor do I.

"What's going on?" Blake demanded.

"I'm able to communicate with Nakeisha, mind to mind," Chaney told him. At the look of surprise on the three faces around him, he continued. "Don't ask me how—it's as surprising to us as it is to you."

"Is she all right?" Vida asked.

"Yes. She's being held in another part of the building, waiting for a senior officer to arrive to question her."

"We need to figure out a way to escape before that happens," Libby said.

I do not know if that will be possible, Nakeisha said. *There are a great many of them.*

Chaney repeated what she said to the others.

"Any ideas?" he asked.

"These floors are dirt," Libby said. "Would it be possible to dig our way out?"

Captain Blake went over to the outside wall and ran his hands along the seams where the stones met, checking for any weaknesses. Scraping away a thin layer of the dirt on the floor, he shook his head.

"These stones are too solid," he said. "And the dirt has rock underneath."

What about your wind? Chaney asked Nakeisha. *Do you still have access to the wind?*

Of course, the wind is with me always.

He smiled as a sudden breeze swirled around him, caressing his face.

"Where'd that draft come from?" Libby asked.

"From Nakeisha," Chaney told her.

"Really? But how—"

Chaney held up a hand for silence so he could concentrate.

Could you use your wind like a weapon, blast down the doors?

He could feel her hesitation before she answered. *It would be a dangerous thing to attempt. I would need to create a small whirlwind and then direct it towards the door. The room I am in is too small for such a thing.*

Chaney relayed what he'd been discussing to the others.

"We need a diversion," Vida said thoughtfully.

"And just what do we have in here that could distract anyone long enough for us to get away?" Blake asked.

"I might have a solution," Chaney said

Is it possible for you to create a wind storm around the town? he asked Nakeisha.

Yes, but to what purpose? They would only raise the shield.

How about two separate storms? One outside the shield, and a stronger one inside the shield.

Nakeisha thought it over. *Yes, it should be simple enough.*

"Nakeisha will be able to provide a distraction to draw the guards away, but we still need a way to get through the door."

Libby bit her lip, then sighed in resignation. "I might be able to help with that."

The others looked at her in surprise. "I don't make a habit of letting it be known, but I'm quite skilled when it comes to opening locks," she admitted.

"I'm getting too old for this," Blake muttered.

"I'd need a wire or a small blade."

"How about this?" Vida asked, unhooking one of her hoop earrings. "If we straightened it out would it be big enough?"

"Maybe if I used both of them," Libby said, turning the earring around in her hand. "They should do fine."

Vida unhooked the other earring and handed it over.

"All right, Chaney," Blake said. "How soon can Nakeisha provide our distraction?"

Chaney relayed the question.

After the intensity of the storm yesterday, it will take at least an hour to build up enough power for a decent sized storm. I will create storm outside the city first. Once it is in place I can draw on it to fuel the storm inside the shield.

Again, Chaney relayed the message.

"Then I guess we sit tight until she gets the guards away," Blake said. "But as soon as they're gone, we'll need to work quickly."

The room Nakeisha was in might have been a pantry at one time, but the shelves lining one of the walls were empty. There were not even any benches or chairs to sit on, so she sat cross-legged on the floor. Relaxing into one of her meditation postures, she reached out with her mind and began drawing on the elemental energy around her.

In a relatively short time the storm klaxon sounded, signaling the raising of the shield. Still Nakeisha drew power towards her. Releasing the storm outside of the shield, she allowed it to run its own course. Now she concentrated on creating the storm within the shield.

She began with a small whirlwind at the far side of the town then split it into three, keeping one in place and sending the other two towards the space port. These two she kept small, but increased their power so they would do the most damage.

You had best hurry, she whispered in Chaney's mind. *I do not know how long the guards will be distracted.*

"All right Libby," Chaney said. "It's now or never."

Libby went over to the lock and studied it carefully. Kneeling down on the floor she straightened out the wire earrings and inserted them, one at a time, into the lock. The others waited impatiently, not wanting to distract her as she moved them around with a delicate touch. At last she reached up and turned the door handle.

"Good work," Blake told her.

She straightened up and held the wires out to Vida. "Would you like your earrings back?" she asked with a grin.

Vida grimaced. "At least they weren't expensive."

"Looks like everything's clear," Chaney said, opening the door a crack. "Let's get Nakeisha and get out of here!"

Chapter Twenty-Six

The tavern had been emptied of Alliance troops.

"I can't believe this worked," said Libby.

"We'd better hurry," Vida said. "Curiosity isn't going to keep them away for long."

Nakeisha, where are you? Chaney reached out with his mind but there was only darkness.

"Something's wrong," he said. "Nakeisha's not answering."

"Is there a chance they moved her?" Vida asked.

Chaney shook his head. "I don't think so, she said they were waiting for someone of higher authority to come to question her."

"Through here," Libby suggested. She was standing near a swinging door that led to the tavern's kitchen.

"Vida, keep watch near the door," Captain Blake ordered. "We'll get Nakeisha and then we'll all get out of here."

Vida nodded and moved to a post near the door, easing it open just a crack.

The kitchen was surprisingly large, though long and narrow. Silently, Blake pointed towards a closed door at the half-way point along one wall. Chaney nodded. The door wasn't locked, but before that fully registered with him, he saw Nakeisha, lying on the floor.

Without thought, he and Blake rushed forward. Chaney knelt by her side.

"Is she all right?" the captain asked.

"Of course she's all right," said a voice behind him. "You don't think I'd let anything happen to something worth so much, do you?"

"Nigel!" Chaney spat. He rose to his feet and turned.

The doctor stood in the doorway, a laser pistol pointed at them. "I've been expecting you. What took you so long?"

"What did you do to her?" Chaney demanded.

"Shouldn't the question be, what am I going to do with you?" Nigel countered. "She's of great value to us. You, on the other hand, have outlived your usefulness."

"How long have you been a spy for the Alliance?" Blake asked, a trace of bitterness in his voice. The ship and crew were his responsibility, how could he have misjudged someone so totally?

"From the beginning," Nigel said proudly. "Tavis and I were both loyal to the Corporate Alliance."

Blake said nothing, though his clenched fists tightened.

"My people have a word for creatures such as yourself," Chaney said.

"Your people," Nigel sneered. "Barbaric savages resistant to change. And the rest of you, bleeding hearts out to save the universe from making a profit."

"A profit made from exploiting worlds that have no defenses!"

The doctor shrugged. "That's their problem then, isn't it? If they're too lazy or stupid to defend themselves, why shouldn't we profit by them?"

"What about Nakeisha," Chaney said, trying a different tact. "She's innocent in all this."

"Innocent? I think not, my naive friend. Her people would make powerful allies for the Alliance."

"After this? You really think they'd ally with someone like you?"

"Maybe not all of them, but enough will. They just need the right incentive. Just like she'll need the right incentive to tell me all her secrets - about the Ilezie, where her home world is, anything I want to know."

"She'll die before she tells you anything," Chaney said with quiet assurance.

"No, she'll just wish she had," Nigel said.

He was so self-assured that Chaney felt a cold chill run up his spine. The people the doctor had allied himself with had already broken so many laws of decency and humanity, what tortures would Nakeisha be subjected to before they were done with her?

All at once, Nigel's body jerked and his eyes widened. A trickle of blood trailed from his open mouth, but he made no sound. The pistol fell from his nerveless fingers and he sank slowly to the ground, a look of surprise on his face.

Libby stood framed in the doorway, a grim expression on her face. "You always did dismiss me as unimportant, Nigel. Guess you won't be dismissing me ever again."

Chaney and the captain looked from Libby to the body with the large kitchen knife sticking out of its back and back to Libby. Under other circumstances, the look of astonishment on their faces might almost have been comical.

"We should probably get moving, just in case he wasn't alone," she suggested.

Chaney ducked back into the depths of the pantry and returned with Nakeisha slung over his shoulder. It was only with great effort that he resisted the urge to kick Nigel's body as he stepped over it, just to make sure he was really dead.

The door to the kitchen swung open.

"There's a squadron of Alliance troops headed towards the tavern," Vida reported.

"There are more knives here," Libby said. "We could arm ourselves and make a stand."

"It's a thought," the captain agreed, "But I don't like the odds of knives against lasers. It couldn't hurt to take a few with us though."

They chose their weapons from the work counter. Captain Blake and Chaney picked up large butcher knives, Libby favored a long, thin, boning knife, and Vida armed herself with an enormous meat cleaver.

"Let's go everyone," the captain said.

He led the way out through the back door into an alley. It was their good fortune that either no one had thought to post a guard here or that the guards had deserted their post because of the storm.

"That's odd," Libby said.

"What's odd?" asked Vida.

"Nothing," she flushed. "It's just the storm sounded much worse from inside the tavern."

Chaney looked around them. "You're right. It looks like it's losing strength."

"Then we'd better hurry," said Vida. "Which way?"

"We don't have a prayer of making it to the Comet," Libby said.

"We could steal an air-car," said Chaney. "And head out into the desert."

"This way then," the captain directed.

The alley opened up close to the network of narrow streets that made up the core of the town. Between the dust swirling around because of the wind and the twisting of the streets, it was an easy task to avoid the patrols. By the time they reached the merchant who rented out the air-cars, the wind had lessened considerably.

Chaney laid Nakeisha carefully in the largest air-car. She was pale, but then she was always pale. Her breathing seemed normal and he couldn't see any obvious injuries. He was pretty sure Nigel drugged her but the question was, what kind of drug?

"What about our wrist-bands?" Vida asked suddenly.

"I have another idea," Chaney said. He leaned back into the air-car and removed the band from Nakeisha's limp wrist. "Everyone give me theirs as well."

When he collected the tracking bands, he went over to another air-car. Tossing them into the back, he made some adjustments on the control panel. The car roared to life and he backed out of it.

"What about the—"

A warning klaxon sounded and the air above them shimmered as the shield went down.

"Never mind," said Libby, who'd been about to ask about the shield.

"I was counting on that," Chaney said. "The shield is automatic, the sensor relays gauge the strength of the wind and when it gets to a certain level, the shield goes up. When the levels drop below the danger point, it goes down again to save power."

He depressed a button on the inside of the air-car and it shot off into the desert.

"I set it on automatic," he said. "It'll keep going until it either hits something or runs out of fuel."

"All right, let's go everyone," Captain Blake said. "The sooner we put some distance between us and the Alliance, the easier I'll breathe."

He and Vida climbed into the front of the air-car while Chaney and Libby sat in the back, Nakeisha between them. As soon as everyone was strapped in, the captain headed the air-car out into the desert, maximum speed.

Chapter Twenty-Seven

It had been morning when they were captured and late afternoon when they escaped. As the sun began lowering in the sky, Vida started looking for a place to stop for the night. They'd been traveling for hours, changing direction at random every hour or so. They settled beside a cluster of boulders that offered some protection from the ever-present breeze.

"Has there been any change in Nakeisha's condition?" Captain Blake asked.

"No sir," Chaney said. He didn't have to add that he was becoming worried.

"Why don't we just leave her in the back of the air-car," the captain told him. "She'll be more comfortable than she would be on the hard ground. There's probably enough room for you to stay with her as well."

Chaney glanced up at him. "Thank you, sir."

"How is she?" Vida asked as the captain joined her.

She and Libby had set up a crude camp in the lee
of the boulders. There wasn't much to it - there was
no wood for a fire, no blankets to make bedrolls.
They had, however, found a supply of food in the air-
car. It appeared the car had been scheduled to be
taken out for a trip.

"No change," he replied. "I don't like it. We have
no idea what Nigel did to her."

"It can't be too serious," Libby said thoughtfully.
"They were still waiting to question her so he
wouldn't have done anything that would cause her
lasting harm."

"This is true," Vida agreed. "He might have slipped
her something to make her unconscious so she
wouldn't escape, intending to revive her for the questioning."

"Let's just hope whatever it is wears off on its
own."

They spent an uneasy night amongst the boulders,
the sighing wind serenading them to sleep. Chaney
stayed with Nakeisha while the others stayed close together to share body heat.

As the sun was beginning to rise, Chaney was over-
joyed to see Nakeisha stir at last. He was on his knees
beside her as she opened her eyes.

She smiled faintly. "Chaney."

"I am here, *fahrois*."

"Where–" she frowned, trying to sort out her
muddled thoughts. "Help me sit up."

He did as she asked, moving to sit beside her on the seat. Her eyes widened slightly as she took in her surroundings. "We escaped?"

"Yes, the wind you created gave us the chance we needed."

She seemed to have trouble focusing. "Why do I feel so strange?"

"It was that *kitak* Nigel. He drugged you. Do you remember?"

"Not really," she shook her head slightly. "There was something . . ."

"You might just need some time for whatever he gave you to work its way out of your system." He hugged her close. "You had me worried."

"I'm sorry. I—"

He quickly put a finger over her lips to silence her. "Don't be. It wasn't your fault. Do you think you could eat something? It might make you feel better."

Nakeisha thought about it for a second, then smiled. "Yes, I definitely think I could eat something."

They joined the others, who were just taking stock of the remaining food. Libby gave in to her impulse and hugged her.

"I was so afraid we hadn't got to you in time."

"And I was afraid that my little storms would not be an effective distraction," Nakeisha said.

"So what now?" Chaney asked. "We've escaped from the Alliance, but where do we go?"

"There's another town," Blake said. "But the Alliance probably has it covered by now."

"What about one of the mines?" Vida suggested. "They should at least have long range communications, we could call for assistance."

"That sounds like a good–" Chaney broke off as Nakeisha suddenly paled. "What's wrong?"

Her eyes were huge in her face. "It's my wind," she said. "I have lost my wind."

Captain Blake uncorked the bottle he found in the air car and gave the contents a sniff. He took a cautious sip and grimaced in satisfaction. It was definitely some kind of whiskey. Glancing up, he saw that Chaney had led Nakeisha over to the shelter of the boulders. Vida and Libby stood helplessly nearby and he joined them.

"Here," he said, handing Chaney the bottle. "This might help."

Chaney knelt down beside Nakeisha. She was staring, unblinking, into the distance. "Please, *fahrois*, try and drink some of this, it will help calm you."

Obediently she took a drink, sputtering as the strong taste of the whiskey hit her taste buds. It seemed to revive her a bit and Chaney coaxed her into taking another sip.

"Can you talk about what happened?" he asked her. "What did Nigel do to you?"

Nakeisha looked at him, shuddering slightly as the fiery liquor hit her bloodstream. She opened her mouth to speak, then took another drink instead. Finally, she seemed to gather herself and took a deep breath.

"It was after we had spoken, mind to mind. I was concentrating on building the wind storms. I didn't realize anyone had entered the room with me."

"Nigel?" Vida guessed.

"Yes. He grabbed me by the arm and demanded to know what I was doing. He said he knew all about my ability to control the wind and if I didn't end the storms he'd end them for me."

"How did he find out?" Chaney asked with a frown.

Nakeisha paused to take another sip from the bottle. "I do not know. I did not admit to anything, of course, but he grew angrier with every passing moment. He told me I'd regret ever crossing him, that he had had more than enough time to come up with a plan to counter my winds."

"What happened then?"

"Then he showed me the syringe he was holding. We struggled, but he was much stronger than he looked. He jabbed me with the needle and that's the last I remember until waking up here," tears filled her eyes, "without my wind."

Chaney pulled her into his arms and let her cry on his shoulder. "It will be all right, *fahrois*. We will find a way to reconnect you with your wind."

Libby went back over to the air-car and returned with the emergency kit. She crouched down beside Nakeisha and Chaney and opened the kit. It took her a moment to find what she was looking for, but finally she held up a small, hand held, medical scanner.

"I figured from the size of the ship there'd be one of these included," she said.

Switching it on, she skimmed it a few inches above Nakeisha's body. Checking the readout, Libby frowned, scanning Nakeisha again.

"What does it say?" Chaney asked.

"He used some kind of inhibitor on her," Libby said hesitantly. "I can't determine how long it will last."

Vida looked over her shoulder. "The good news is that it was definitely a drug of some kind."

"How is that good news?" the captain asked.

"It's good because a drug isn't permanent. If it doesn't wear off, it can be counter-acted."

"It is like there is a piece of me missing," Nakeisha murmured against Chaney's shoulder. "Like my soul has been ripped away."

"We will get through this," he told her.

"Vida is right," Captain Blake said, taking charge once more. "Whatever Nigel has done, we can find a way to undo it. In the meantime we need to plan our next move."

Chapter Twenty-Eight

Nakeisha allowed herself a few more minutes of comfort in Chaney's arms before pulling away. "We should keep moving," she said. "The longer we stay in one place, the greater the chances they'll find us."

"Are you sure you're alright?" Chaney asked.

She dredged up a smile for him. "I am sorry if I worried you. I am more myself now."

He eyed her skeptically. "I think—"

"Vida is correct. Whatever Nigel did to me can undoubtedly be undone. I was born an Ardraci, there is nothing that can take that away from me."

"In that case," the captain said, "I suggest we get under way. We'll make for the nearest mine and try and get a message to the council."

Chaney plotted the course and in minutes they were underway.

"How far is it to the mine?" Vida asked.

"It should only take us a couple of hours, three at the most," Chaney told her.

He would have preferred Vida to be piloting the craft so he could sit with Nakeisha, but she'd insisted on him taking his turn. Every time he thought of what Nigel did to Nakeisha, his anger returned. With an effort he calmed himself. The man was dead. It's not like he had the power to resurrect him so he could kill him again.

Chaney, can you hear me? He started as the voice whispered through his mind.

Nakeisha?

He felt her amusement. *And who else would be speaking to you, mind to mind?*

Is everything all right?

Yes, I just wanted to make sure this connection had not been blocked as well.

I'm relieved it isn't.

I am pleased as well, she replied. Then, after a moment, *It is a shame that Libby killed him.*

Why is that? He asked, surprised.

Because now he cannot be questioned about the drug he used. Was it his own creation? Is it something the Alliance is aware of? If there is a drug that can block my people's connection to their element, it is my duty to find out what it is.

Well I'm not sorry he's dead, although I would have preferred killing him myself.

"I have something on the sensors," Captain Blake said. "It's too big to be an Alliance ship, it must be the mine. We should have a visual in a few minutes."

"There!" Libby pointed over their shoulders.

The mine was as grey and depressing looking as the rest of the planet, nestled in a cluster of rocky hills. There were several outbuildings built of local stone, and four large warehouses set back from the mine itself. There was no sign of life, nor did anyone come out to greet them as Chaney landed the air-car. There did not even appear to be any vehicles around.

"I thought all the mines were operational," Vida said.

"I thought so too." Captain Blake looked around uneasily.

"Could they have depleted the ore here," Nakeisha asked, "and moved on to a more profitable location?"

"It doesn't look like it's been closed down," the captain replied. "More like it was abandoned in a hurry."

"Maybe the Alliance scared them off," Libby suggested. "Or rounded them up."

"That's more likely," Blake agreed. "All right, everyone stay together. My gut's telling me that something's going on here and I always trust my gut. Let's go find that communications station."

Everywhere they looked there were signs of people leaving in a hurry – papers scattered in the offices, meals half eaten in the dining hall, personal possessions abandoned. The communications center was in the third building they checked.

Libby sat down at the controls and flipped a few switches. Frowning, she toggled one of the switches back and forth a few times and then tried typing a command into the system's computer.

"It's no use sir," she said, turning around. "The system's dead."

"*Kiesh'nafi*," Vida said succinctly as the small group stared at the useless communications panel.

The Alliance was going to catch up with them sooner or later; getting a message out to the Council was their only hope of surviving. There were, of course, other mines they could send a signal from, but the air-car was too low on fuel to consider trying to make any but the shortest of hops. This had been their last chance.

"Cap," Chaney said. "Let me take a look at it. I know a bit about electronics. I might be able to cobble something together."

"The rest of us can strip the air-car of parts," Vida suggested. "There should be something Chaney could use."

"All right," the captain agreed. "Let's go."

The silence of the mining compound was a little unnerving. Everything was still, sheltered as they were there wasn't even the ever-present breeze. Vida wasted no time when they reached the air-car. She climbed inside and started taking apart the main console. Libby and Nakeisha looked at each other and then Nakeisha spoke.

"I do not know of what use I can be," she said apologetically. "I know nothing of electronics or what might be useful."

"And I can operate a communications grid, but I don't know the first thing about repairing one," Libby admitted.

"In that case, why don't you two go back to the dining hall and see if you can find some food," the captain suggested. "Even if we do get a message out, we'll probably be stuck here a while."

Libby and Nakeisha picked their way carefully through the rubble of discarded equipment on their way to the dining hall.

"They appear to have left in a great hurry," Nakeisha observed.

Several tables held the remains of half-eaten meals. Libby picked up one of the plates. She touched the food on it then brought the plate closer to give it a sniff.

"This can't be more than three, four hours old."

"It could not have been an attack," Nakeisha said thoughtfully.

Libby looked at her. "What makes you say that?"

She shrugged. "There is no sign of a struggle. No bodies, not even any blood."

"But they certainly left in a hurry," Libby said, putting the plate down again. "Let's check back here," she motioned to a set of double doors at the end of the room.

The kitchen wasn't in any better shape. The stoves had been turned off, but partially filled pots and pans still sat on the burners.

"You would think a mining facility would have heating units instead of these old things," Libby said, running her hand along the edge of a stove.

"Perhaps they save their improvements for the mine itself," Nakeisha said absently. "What do you suppose caused this?"

She was looking at a large bowl, overflowing with a grey, foamy substance.

"I have no idea," Libby said, looking over her shoulder. "I don't see any food processing units, but the cooler is fully stocked." She shivered. "This place gives me the creeps. Let's get out of here."

Nakeisha heartily agreed. They returned to the communications center.

Chaney had the console in pieces and his brow was furrowed in concentration as he stared at it. Vida and the captain had an arm load of electronics from the air-car and Nakeisha and Libby were pleased to report that although the dining hall had been abandoned in a hurry, there was still plenty of food in storage.

They tried not to stare at Chaney as he worked, but there was very little else to look at. He ignored them, for the most part, save for the occasional request for a tool or a part. At last he sat back with a frown.

"What is it?" Nakeisha asked, resting her hand on his shoulder. He reached up and covered her hand with his own.

"All that's lacking now is a power source."

"What kind of power source do you need?" Blake asked.

"The stronger the better if we're planning on being able to contact our allies."

The captain gestured to the pile of stripped components. "We have the batteries from the air-car, would they be any use?"

"Not strong enough," Chaney told him.

"Look at that," Vida said in wonder, pointing to where Nakeisha's hand still rested on Chaney's shoulder.

"What is that?" Libby asked. There was a blue thread of electricity crawling over Nakeisha's fingers.

Nakeisha looked down in surprise. "It . . . is difficult to explain."

"Something about being out in the storm affected us," Chaney said slowly. "I don't know why it's happening now."

Chapter Twenty-Nine

Chaney turned in his chair and laced his fingers with Nakeisha's. The blue fire twisted around their joined hands. "Can you feel a storm approaching?"

She frowned in concentration, "I can almost sense something," then shook her head, "but I do not know what it is."

"Could someone check outside?"

"I'll go," Vida said.

"Does it hurt?" Libby asked, taking a step closer. She reached out and touched their joined hands. There was a snapping, crackling sound and she jerked her hand backwards. "Ow!"

Nakeisha and Chaney looked her in astonishment. "Are you all right?"

"I'm fine," Libby said, cradling her hand. "Just a slight singe, the shock's already fading. What about you two?"

"It doesn't harm us at all," Chaney told her. "There's no pain, it just —" he glanced at Nakeisha and she blushed. "It just tickles."

"The wind's starting to pick up outside," Vida reported. "Looks like you're right, Chaney. There's another storm on the way."

"Will we be safe in here?" Nakeisha asked.

"These buildings are sturdier than the ones in town," Vida assured her.

"That's true," Captain Blake agreed, "But I think we should find someplace more secure to wait out the storm."

"What about the mine?" Libby asked. They all turned to look at her. "The tunnels would go deep underground. Surely we'd be safe there."

"An excellent idea," the captain said. "Let's go."

"Wait, captain," Chaney said. "What about the message?"

"We can't worry about that now, we'll just have to figure out something once the storm's over."

"If you took this portable communicator, then you should be able to send a message from inside the mine, once we find a power source for the communications grid."

"But we don't have a power source," the captain said impatiently. "We need to get moving."

"With all due respect, sir, we do have a power source." He held up his hand, still holding Nakeisha's, blue-white lines of energy dancing around their twined fingers. He looked at her for permission and she nodded. "Something happened to us when we were out in the desert," he said. "I don't now exactly what it was, but when there's a storm approaching we seem to . . . generate energy between us. Whether we want to or not."

"And you think you two will generate enough power to get a message out?"

"I know we will sir. Especially if we stay up here."

"Are you crazy?"

"No sir. As Vida pointed out, these buildings are much sturdier than the ones in town. And the closer we are to the storm, the more energy will build up between us."

"I don't like it. It's too dangerous."

"It is imperative that we get a message to the Council," Nakeisha said. "I believe that Chaney and I will be in little danger from the storm, even without being able to control the wind I can still keep it at bay. As for the energy – it is a risk I am willing to take."

"Are you sure you can't create this energy down in the mine?"

She shook her head. "I believe the energy is drawn from the magnetic force of the storms themselves. If we were cut off from the storm, as we would be in the mine, we would also be cut off from the energy."

"All right," the captain said heavily. "I'll agree that you can give it a try. But if it's not working, or you think you're in any danger, I want you down in the mine with the rest of us."

"Aye, sir," Chaney said.

After the others left, Chaney pulled Nakeisha into his arms. The energy flared to life.

"If I did not know better, I would accuse you of contriving this situation just so we could spend time alone together."

"I'm sorry to say I'm not quite that devious," he told her. "Are you sure you want to attempt this? After what happened the last time . . ."

"Have you not noticed that the energy also heightens desire? Even were we not attempting to power the communications net I would want to do this."

He pulled her closer, brushing his lips over hers. Lines of blue energy curled around them. The storm outside was building in strength, but they took no notice.

"You promised me a nice, soft, bed," Nakeisha admonished.

"How about a well-worn sofa?"

Chaney released her long enough to duck into the outer room and drag in the sofa from the lounge area. Nakeisha eyed it dubiously.

"Perhaps the floor would be safer."

"Where's your sense of adventure?" He swept her up in his arms and laid her on the sofa. "Now, where were we?"

She reached up, tracing his face with one finger, leaving a trail of fiery blue on his skin. "I believe we were about to create a power source for the captain."

Nakeisha laid her palm over Chaney's cheek creating a blue static crackle. He shivered at the sensation and brought his face closer, lips hovering over hers. The energy arced between them. She cried out as pleasure shafted through her, the sound lost as his mouth came down hard on hers.

Whimpering in the back of her throat, her hands worked frantically at the fastenings of his shirt. She ached for skin to skin contact. He helped her peel his shirt away and then searched out the fastenings of her robe while she went to work on his pants.

"Hurry," she gasped. "I cannot wait!"

"I'm trying," he said, feeling every bit as frantic as she was.

The lines of bright blue snaked over their skin, writhing and twisting around them. Chaney tried to slow down, to love her the way she deserved, but the threads of energy made the slightest touch between them almost unbearably pleasurable. He quivered under the strain of trying to hold back.

"Please," she begged.

Her hands seemed to be everywhere, running over his chest, along his shoulders, pulling him closer. She made it impossible to resist. He growled, slamming into her, the sensation sending a shiver through his whole body. The light from the blue energy intensified into an almost burning glow.

Everywhere she touched him she left a fiery trail of blue sparks in her wake. Chaney struggled to hold back, to keep from hurting her, but Nakeisha did not want slow and gentle. She wanted, needed, fast and hard.

"More," she gasped. "I need more."

Incapable of further speech, she used her mouth and her hands to urge him on. He was helpless to refuse. Fueled by both her need and his own he quickened the pace. The blue fire turned their bodies into one, complete, erogenous zone.

Around them the controls of the communications center began to light up, powered by the energy building between them. They were oblivious to anything but each other and their insatiable desire. Nakeisha's breath came in sobbing gasps, her legs wrapped tightly around him, hands clawing at his back to try and bring him closer. Chaney surged into her, knowing on some level there was something wrong about this but unable to stop.

The energy, like their desire, continued to build until it reached its peak. Chaney and Nakeisha cried out together, reaching completion in a burst of blue white light. The communications console exploded in a shower of sparks, and went dead.

Chaney stirred, and groaned. Carefully he levered his weight off Nakeisha. Her eyes flickered and opened. She smiled wanly up at him. "I would wish very much not to have to move for several days."

"I agree," he said, wincing as he sat up properly. "I hurt all over." He helped her sit up beside him.

"Your back!" she exclaimed, catching sight of the bloody furrows. "I cannot believe I did that to you!"

He caught her hands in his and kissed her knuckles. "It's nothing, really. I hardly even feel it."

She looked at him dubiously but he remained firm.

"Was it just my imagination," he said hesitantly, "Or was that more . . . intense . . . than it was when we were out in the desert?"

She nodded in agreement. "It did seem to be stronger. I think, perhaps, we should not do this again while we are on Anchyre."

Chaney sighed. "I'm afraid I have to agree. It's not just that I'm afraid of hurting you, I think the energy build up could do some serious damage."

It took more than an hour before they were re-covered enough to make their way down into the mine where the others waited in the auxiliary control room.

"You look terrible!" Libby blurted out when she saw them. "Are you all right?"

Nakeisha smiled at her tiredly. "We will be fine. More importantly, were you able to send a message?"

"Whatever you two did up there," the captain said, "It worked. We were able to get a short message out. With the burst of energy just before the circuits blew, we might even have been able to reach the Council itself."

Chaney grinned. The color rose in Nakeisha's face and she looked away.

"Captain, you'd better take a look at this," Vida called from another console.

"What is it?"

"I managed to siphon off enough power to get the proximity grid working."

"Is that what I think it is?"

"I'm afraid so, Captain."

Chapter Thirty

The others crowded around the console.

"What is it?" Nakeisha asked.

"An Alliance patrol ship," Libby said bleakly. "And it's headed for the mine."

"Is there any chance the Council could get here first?" Nakeisha asked.

"No," Chaney told her gently. "Even if there was a Council ship in this sector, they wouldn't be close enough to get here before the Alliance."

"This mine is pretty extensive, Cap," Vida said. "Maybe we could hide out further down until the Council gets here."

Nakeisha blanched

"What is it?" Chaney asked.

"I – I cannot," she pulled away from his comforting touch and paced away, whirling around after a few steps. "I cannot go further into the mine. This level is bad enough, but we are not so very deep and it has much the same look as the rooms on the surface."

"Are you saying you're claustrophobic?" Libby asked.

"I am an Elemental," she said helplessly. "My element is the air, I cannot be under the earth for any great length of time."

Chaney went over to her and pulled her into his arms. "You should have said something sooner," he said. "I'd never have made you come down here if I'd known."

"I know this," she said, returning his hug. "I did not think a short stay would pose any difficulties."

"The Alliance may not know for certain that we're here," Libby said thoughtfully. "They might just be checking out the energy surge."

"They'll know the moment they spot the air-car," Vida pointed out.

"Okay," Captain Blake said, thinking furiously. "Here's what we're going to do. First, we go back up to the surface. All of us," he added, when Nakeisha opened her mouth to protest. "We stick together, no matter what."

Nakeisha nodded, too moved to respond. That these people should once again face danger because of her was unconscionable.

"Chaney, was there any power left in the air-car?

"A little, Cap. Not enough to take us too far from here."

"It doesn't matter. I want you to rig it for automatic like you did the other one. Pick a direction you like and send it off. The rest of us will make sure there's no trace of us being here. With luck they'll think the energy burst was a fluke and move on."

Powering up the air-car meant re-installing the batteries and a few of the other components that had been stripped away. The captain chaffed at the amount of time it took but Vida and Chaney worked together and sent the air-car off. At Vida's suggestion, they sought refuge in the valley formed by the rocks on the north side of the mining complex. The high metal content in the rock made it an effective shield against scans.

Nakeisha stumbled, catching herself on a rock before she fell. Her eyes widened.

"Are you all right?" Chaney asked.

"Here," she guided his hand to the rock. "Do you feel that?"

He looked at her in surprise. "What is that?"

"I believe the metal in these rocks gives them the ability to store energy."

"I wonder if it's connected to what's happening to us?"

"Indeed, but how?"

"I don't know," he admitted. "Maybe it's the rocks that are causing the energy spikes, not the storms."

"It is too bad we did not discover this earlier." She slanted him a teasing glance. "It might have saved your back much injury."

He returned her smile, pleased by her courage, her ability to joke in such a serious situation.

The group managed to conceal themselves just in time. The Alliance ship was smaller than they expected, if they'd been armed they might even have been able to take it. The troops that disembarked were not as well ordered as the ones from the town, and the officer in charge directed them to make a systematic search of the buildings.

"Mercenaries," Vida hissed.

They were so intent watching what was going on in the compound, they failed to notice the troops circling around behind them.

"Hands up," a voice demanded. "Turn around slowly."

Despair washed through Nakeisha like an ocean wave. This was her fault.

A loud explosion came from the other side of the rock and they flinched.

"Don't move!" the squadron leader barked. "You," he nodded to one of the men. "Go get the captain and let him know we have prisoners."

The captain was every bit as scruffy looking as his troops. He was perhaps middle-aged – hair turning grey and the beginnings of a paunch hanging over his belt. His eyes lit up when he saw the prisoners.

"There'll be a bonus for sure, boys," he said. "Take her," he pointed at Nakeisha, "back to the ship and make sure she's good and secure. Shoot the others."

"Captain," the man holding the gun on them said. "It's been a long time since we've come across any women."

"Fine," the captain said impatiently. "Just don't take too long. And kill them when you're done. We've already blown the mine so we need to get moving."

Something in Nakeisha snapped. She took a step forward. Out of nowhere a gust of wind snaked into the valley, swirling around her, lifting her hair in a black nimbus around her head.

Nakeisha?

My wind has returned to me!

"I am Ardraci," she said in a calm, clear voice. "And I say you will not do this thing."

"I don't care if you're Queen of the Universe," the captain said. "I'm in charge here, not you."

Anchor yourself to the rock. The command whispered through Chaney's mind. Without thinking, he reached out and laid a palm on the rock beside him. A flicker of static traveled up his arm.

"No," Nakeisha said gently. "You are not."

The wind suddenly intensified, creating a small whirlwind around the captain that lifted him in the air.

"Shoot her!" the captain screamed.

"I think not." The whirlwind spun him away.

Take my hand, now.

Chaney stretched out his free hand and clasped Nakeisha's. The effect was immediate. Blue fire sprang to life, radiating from their joined hands and crawling up their arms. The guards backed up and raised their weapons.

They had no chance to fire. Through her connection with Chaney, Nakeisha drew energy from the rock and directed it towards the guards. They were thrown back in a burst of crackling blue energy.

"Impressive," Blake said from behind them.

"We might have a bit of a problem, Cap," Chaney said, voice strained. Nakeisha's hand trembled in his as the energy continued to build.

"The others are still searching, now would be an excellent time to take their ship," Nakeisha added.

"All right, let's go."

"You will have to go without us," Nakeisha told him.

"What? Why?"

"I can't seem to let go of this—no!" Chaney shouted as Blake moved to help him. "Don't touch either of us. The energy would fry you. Just go, get out of here."

"But what about you two?" Libby asked. "We can't just leave you here."

"We will be fine," Nakeisha said, not knowing whether she lied or not. "But I do not know how long I can keep the energy from seeking a release. Take the ship and go!"

Captain Blake opened his mouth to speak but then took in her paleness and the lines of strain on her face. Beads of sweat formed on Chaney's forehead.

"How will we know when it's safe to come back for you?"

Chaney attempted to grin; it turned into more of a grimace. "You'll know, Cap. Trust me, you'll know."

He watched as they reluctantly headed for the Alliance ship. They were more than just shipmates, they were his friends. He wondered if he'd ever see them again.

Do you think they'll get far enough away?

I do not know. I do not know that there is any place safe on this world.

They heard the roar of the engines coming to life and watched with a measure of relief as the ship rose into the air and shot, not just away from the mine, but straight upwards into space.

The energy surrounding them was so bright Chaney could no longer make out Nakeisha's features. *This is different than the other times, isn't it?*

Yes, I—Oh, Chaney, I cannot hold it, it burns!

You are my heart, he told her. He tugged her a step closer. *You are my soul and my life.*

You are my beloved, we are joined for always and beyond. She took the final step into the curve of his waiting embrace. The air around them went still.

In a blinding supernova, the energy exploded outwards.

Chapter Thirty-One

Darkness, unrelenting darkness.
Awareness, but no knowledge of self.
Sound, indistinguishable voices.
Touch, by unfamiliar hands.
Pain.
"Watch it! That one almost got me."
"Where's that tranquilizer?"
"Here!"
"Don't just stand there, use it!"
Fade to soothing black.

For Chaney, full awareness came slowly. His mind
was somewhat fogged, as though he'd been asleep for
a very long time. He was lying in a bed; he could feel
the softness beneath him and a covering pulled tight
over him. The air he breathed was clean and fresh –
no longer on the planet then, he must be on a ship.

There was something important he was missing. He struggled to remember.

"I think he's coming round."

"Chaney, can you hear me?"

The first voice was unfamiliar. The second, however . . . Knowledge came flooding back.

"Nakeisha!" His eyes snapped open and he struggled to sit up. Gentle, but familiar, hands held him still.

"Rest easy, beloved. It is over and we are safe."

She leaned down and kissed him.

"You're alive," he said stupidly. "We're alive!" He reached up and pulled her half-down on top of him for another, fiercer kiss.

"Humans!" said the unfamiliar voice, though it was laced with humor.

Nakeisha pushed herself free and helped Chaney to sit up in the bed. Unwilling to let go of her, he tugged her down to sit beside him. With her secure at his side he glanced towards the source of the strange voice and froze.

The creature standing on the other side of the bed was unlike any he'd ever seen, and in his travels he'd seen plenty. Though not overly large in size, the being gave the impression of great stature. Its pale blue skin shimmered under the bright light; it was hairless and wore a nondescript brown robe with the hood thrown back.

It stared back at him just as frankly, large golden eyes filled with humor. "Are you quite finished examining me like a bug under a microscope tribesman?"

"E.Z.?"

"Very good, tribesman. So much quicker than your *enjulla.*"

"I knew you were Ilezie, but the last time I saw you in corporeal form you were green," Nakeisha said peevishly.

"You know very well we are able to change color at will," E.Z. admonished. The blue of his skin faded and was replaced with green, which in turn faded to yellow.

"Stop," Chaney said, closing his eyes as a rainbow of colors began chasing each other across E.Z.'s skin. It made him ill to watch. "What's an *enjulla?*"

"Your life-mate, soul-mate, bonded partner, spouse, consort, wife – take your pick."

Chaney slanted a look at Nakeisha. His eyes widened.

"Your hair!"

She ducked her head, self-conscious. "Yours is the same," she mumbled.

Chaney reached out and wound one iridescent white strand around his fingers. Gently he tugged her head downwards so he could kiss her again.

"It's beautiful," he told her. "It makes you even more beautiful than ever."

"And you as well –"

"If you two are going to start a mating ritual, I'm leaving."

Nakeisha blushed and Chaney grinned. "Where are we?" he asked.

"We are aboard the Valkyrie. And before you ask, your companions were found and are on board as well."

Chaney was rendered speechless. There wasn't a spacer alive who hadn't heard of the Valkyrie, the flagship of the Council fleet. The only ship to have survived the human-Kohl-trin war intact.

"I was able to use the energy you raised while mating in the desert to return to the home world to join with my new body. From there I rendezvoused with the Valkyrie and we came directly here."

"Wait, they had a body waiting for you?" Nakeisha asked. "You were anticipating being killed?"

E.Z. shrugged. "One of the hazards of corporeal form is that no matter how well they're taken care of, they do not last forever. When we feel our form begin to die, we grow a new one and transfer our consciousness before the old one can no longer sustain life."

"And in the case of a sudden death, like yours?"

"Then we must find a host to hold our essence until we can return to the home world. We usually keep several uninhabited forms waiting for just such emergencies."

"How, ah, very foresighted of you," Chaney said. He had the feeling there was a lot more to it than that, but he let it go for now.

"What I am most curious about," Nakeisha said, "Is how we survived the energy blast. I felt the power of it. It was nothing like the previous ones."

"Ah," E.Z. seated himself on the foot of the bed. "That is a tale that will be told for generations. Are you familiar with Kandor and Shinandu?"

"The moons of Anchyre?" Nakeisha asked. "What have they to do with this?"

"I mean the warlord Kandor and Queen Shinandu."

"They were real?" Chaney asked in surprise. "I thought their story was told just to add some local color."

"They were quite real, I assure you. And their story is true, for the most part, though not quite as romantic. Kandor greatly desired Shinandu, but she did not return his feelings. He kidnapped her and took her to his mountain home where he raped her."

"How awful!" Nakeisha said, "But what—"

"What the story does not mention is that Kandor and Shinandu were elementals."

The Ilezie's words hung in the air, the ring of truth undeniable. Nakeisha leaned back weakly against Chaney's supporting arm. "How is that possible?"

"Think you that you are the only elemental to step beyond the bounds of her world?"

She opened her mouth to argue and then changed her mind. "I am sorry. Pray continue."

"Kandor was of the earth and Shinandu of the air, both filled with incredible power. When they fought they caused storms and earthquakes that shook the world. Their joining, forced as it was, did indeed cause a cataclysm that laid waste to the world, stripping Anchyre of life."

"They had the power to do this?"

"Oh, indeed they did. Understand, this happened a very long time ago."

E.Z. paused, choosing his next words carefully.

"It was always believed that given the right set of circumstances, life could return to Anchyre. It would take a great deal of energy, however, and a connection to both the earth and the sky."

Chaney couldn't quite believe what he was hearing. "Are you trying to say we caused another cataclysm? One that put the entire planet to rights again?"

"I would not, perhaps, call it a cataclysm, but essentially you are correct."

"But Chaney is not an elemental, how is this possible?"

"Through him, you were able to connect to the earth, to draw the energy back out of the rock where Kandor sent it. Your own elemental power cleared away the storms that laid waste to the land. For the first time in more than a thousand years, it is raining on Anchyre."

Nakeisha stared at him in astonishment. It was too unfathomable for her to wrap her mind around.

"Well," Chaney said, once the silence had stretched out for several minutes. "At the very least it will make an interesting tale to tell our children."

"Your child will be an entirely new elemental," E.Z. told them proudly. "He will be born of the energy you shared."

Chaney and Nakeisha looked at each other blankly, then back at him.

"Child?" Chaney ventured.

"Child?" Nakeisha echoed. Her hand went to her flat abdomen.

"Did you think that all that coupling would be without consequence?" E.Z. shook his head in amusement. "You children make me feel old."

"Just how old are you?" Nakeisha asked.

"As old as I need to be," E.Z. said, smiling serenely. He rose gracefully to his feet. "And now, dear children, I must leave."

"You don't just mean leaving the room, do you?" Chaney asked.

"Very astute, tribesman. It seems I am needed elsewhere. There have been rumors . . ." he shrugged. "But they are of no consequence. What matters is that my task here is done."

Tears filled Nakeisha's eyes. "Is that all I was? A task to be completed?"

"You know better than that," E.Z. admonished gently. He moved closer and caught a single teardrop on his long finger. "I will tell you a secret. There is a reason the Ilezie became guardians to the Ardraci."

He moved away from them and began to glow faintly. "We are not able to produce offspring, the Ardraci filled that void for us. You are truly the child of my heart. You both are."

"Does this mean we will see you again?"

E.Z.'s glow intensified. "Of a certainty, I would not miss the birth of my god son and daughter." His form grew more insubstantial.

"Wait!" Chaney yelled as his words sank in. "Son and daughter? We're having twins?"

E.Z.'s laughter floated behind him as he disappeared. "You two never seem to do anything by halves."

"Twins," Chaney repeated, stunned.

"Kandor and Shinandu," Nakeisha mused.

An excellent choice, the whisper went through their minds simultaneously. *Your offspring will bring great honor to those names again.*

"Well, I guess that's settled then," Chaney said.

"Twins," Nakeisha said, shaking her head. "I do not think I have ever heard of an Ardraci giving birth to twins before."

"Do you know what I just realized?"

"What?" Nakeisha turned to look at him, heart quickening at the look in his eye.

He pulled her down lower in the bed. "We're out of danger and we're alone in a nice, soft, bed."

"We are going to be parents," Nakeisha said, as his hands went to the fastenings of her robe.

"Yes we are. I think that's cause to celebrate, don't you?"

"Oh, yes!"

And celebrate they did.

About the Author

Residing in Cobourg, Ontario, Carol has always had a love of writing. She grew up reading old copies of Edgar Rice Burroughs and Robert E. Howard so it's no wonder her first love is fantasy and science fiction.

She always believed she was meant to be a writer of short stories, however her stories tended to be rather long. They also tended to have a romantic thread running through them. Finally caving in to the inevitable, she embraced her genre of began writing novels of fantasy/science fiction adventure with a dash of romance thrown into the mix. She has never regretted it.

Today she writes a variety of prose: non-fiction, flash fiction, short stories, and novels – in a variety of genres: humour, horror, contemporary, romance, science fiction, and fantasy. Having recently discovered a love of poetry forms, she explores a new form of poetry every week.

Visit Carol on her blog, <u>Random Thoughts of the Writerly Kind.</u>